CRABS
OMNIBUS

A selection of recent titles by Guy N. Smith

www.guynsmith.com
@guynsmith

Crabs Omnibus

GUY N SMITH

BLACK HILL
BOOKS

First Published in Paperback format by
Black Hill Books, England, August 2015.

First Published in eBook format by
Black Hill Books, England, September 2015.

FIRST EDITION

ISBN: 1907846883
ISBN-13: 978-1-907846-88-5

For Shane Agnew, a very good friend and a long-time fan of the Crabs.

Guy

CONTENTS

INTRODUCTION

1976 was the year in which my life underwent a complete change. For the past twenty years I had been attempting to find a means of getting out of banking and establishing a lifestyle far removed from the 9-5 routine which denied me creativity. I had already written many short stories, magazine articles and had had three horror novels published but these were not sufficient for me to risk the precarious enterprise of self-employment.

Then New English Library published my 'Night of the Crabs' which was set on the Welsh coast around the delightful holiday resort of Barmouth where I had been holidaying for a couple of years with my wife and four young children.

I believed that 'Night of the Crabs' would be just another novel with good but modest sales. Realization of its impetus within the genre came about one balmy, summer evening when we were meandering through the town of Barmouth. In those days shops stayed open late and I wandered into the local W H Smiths.

I stared in disbelief at the scene which greeted me, a revolving rack crammed with my latest novel. An excited shout went up from my kids 'Dad, they're selling loads of your books!' Heads turned in the crowded shop and the manager approached me. The outcome was that I ended up doing a signing session, an unbelievable turn of events which was to escalate in the coming months.

NEL advertised 'Night of the Crabs' as 'The No.1 Beach Read' and so it proved to be – for those who had the courage to lie on sun-drenched beaches in that glorious summer of record breaking temperatures with the prospect of crabs as big as cows emerging from the tide, hell-bent on destruction, dismemberment and a feast of human flesh!

Within weeks the film rights had been purchased by Milton Subotski of Amicus Films. Sadly Milton died soon afterwards and I heard nothing more of my movie until it appeared on late night TV in the 1980s.

In the meantime, though, reprints of the book came thick and fast and NEL demanded a sequel. So I wrote 'Killer Crabs' set on Australia's Great Barrier Reef.

The Crabs soon had a cult following and reprints of novels now carried a 'by the author of Night of the Crabs' bold announcement on their covers. Five further sequels followed along with some short stories. Translation rights sold around the world, including the USA where the books featured some stunning embossed covers.

All this enabled me to fulfil my ambition of retiring from banking and moving with my family to live in a remote area of the Shropshire/Welsh border hills. Here I was able to pursue my rural hobbies and to write a further 80 or so books. I am still writing.

Thus I owe a lot to the Crabs and to those fans who bought the books. I will never take them for granted.

Four decades on the Crabs are still going strong. Thus I decided to put together a volume of short stories, five of which have already been published, some several years ago, together with a couple of originals. This omnibus edition is principally for the completist collector. If he, or she, has all the novels then this book will complete the long history of those terrible crustaceans.

I am repeatedly asked if there will be further crab chronicles. Well, it all depends upon whether or not they have finally been wiped out or is there still a pregnant female lurking somewhere in the depths of the ocean ready to spawn a new generation of human-hungry monsters. Just as mankind has been attempting to render them extinct so are the crabs hell-bent on the total destruction of human life on earth.

Truthfully, I do not know if my crustaceans will return. Along with my readership I can only wait and see.

CRUSTACEAN CARNAGE

Far from its ocean home a crab feeds on human victims as it embarks upon a return journey to the coast

1

"Christ, this one feels like a block of bloody concrete!" Elwyn Jones heaved on the rope of the sunken crab pot, took the strain until beads of sweat stood out on his grizzled features. "It must've got stuck on sommat, can't shift the bugger. You'll 'ave to give me a hand, Ade."

Adrian Summers eased his lanky frame up off the bench seat on the opposite side of the small fishing boat. He had been travelling down to the Welsh coast on and off for the past ten years to accompany his old friend on these trips to haul in a line of crab/lobster pots, sometimes fishing for mackerel whilst the other collected his catches. Such excursions during the winter months were few and far between with rough seas frequent. This week, though, in spite of a spell of bitterly cold weather, the tides were moderate.

"Hang on, I'll be right with you," Adrian grasped the rope, braced himself. "God knows what you've caught in this one, Elwyn. Ah, it's coming now."

Slowly, surely, the vessel broke the surface, came into view.

"What the bloody hell is that hanging on to it?" He gasped.

"A crab, the biggest I've seen in these waters!" The veins were standing out on the older man's forehead. "Let's get it on board and 'ave a look at it."

Slowly the pot and its passenger were dragged up over the side, hit the deck with a resounding thump and rolled. The crab was dislodged, lay there.

"It looks dead to me," Adrian grunted, breathing heavily. "Drifted in with the tide, somehow got tangled up on the pot with its claws."

"No, it ain't dead," the fisherman stooped, regarded his catch closely. "Sort of … slumbering. Crabs don't hibernate, they usually head for deep waters in cold like this. I reckon this one didn't make it out there so it went into a kind of somnolent state. It would probably have died in a day or two. But what the devil is it? It's almost like one of them Japanese Spider Crabs but not quite. We don't get them here, anyway. Wait a minute …" He bent closer. "It's no ordinary crab, that goes without saying. And … and it's a youngster, just a baby!"

"You mean it could grow even bigger?"

"If it's what I'm thinking, Ade, then I don't like the look of it at all. Not one little bit. I could be wrong, I hope I am for everybody's sake on this coastline."

"Go on, tell me the bad news, Elwyn." Adrian stepped back a pace.

"I'm going back forty years. I was just a kid then and you weren't even born, but doubtless you've heard about the crab attack on Barmouth."

"I've heard stories, didn't believe half of them, but there has to be something in them."

"Sure was. Saw some for myself once. Awesome. They reckon they were the result of some underwater nuclear testing. Whatever, it was a virtual war. The armed forces thought they'd eliminated 'em but they turned up a time or two afterwards; Scotland, East Coast and some down under. Never could be certain that the last one was dead. Only needed a female somewhere to keep on breeding the bastards."

"And …"

"I think this bugger is one of their babies which means they're still out there somewhere, hopefully far away. Somehow this one didn't make it back to wherever they're hiding. Went into a kind of sleepy state but still needed to eat. The eels in the pot attracted it but it couldn't get to them, fell asleep clinging to the pot. And now we've got it here on board, harmless at the moment but if it woke then I reckon it could cause mayhem, take your arm or leg off with those pincers. Just look at 'em! Problem is what are we going to do with it. If we dump it back in the sea it could well find its way back to its mamma, that's if it doesn't die in the meantime. Or do we leave it somewhere on dry land and hope that it dies? I don't want to invite any publicity myself, can't be doing with the bloody press queuing up to interview me, photos in the papers and all that kind of crap."

"I've got an idea," Adrian pursed his lips.

"Let's hear it then."

"As you know I've got a fishing tackle shop in Lichfield. At my home in Hilton, about three miles from the city, I'm developing a commercial trout fishing business. My pool is about an acre in size and the fish won't be arriving until later in the year."

"So you want to take this bloody crab home with you and put it in your pool. I get your idea. Jesus wept! Well, if it stays there then you won't have any trout left."

"How long do you think it can survive in fresh water, Elwyn?"

"Dunno. Those big 'uns, after Barmouth, turned up in rivers, inland lochs etc. They're different. But what about when it grows? They grow fast. You'll have a dangerous monster on your hands."

"I'm thinking there's a deal in it for both of us, a fifty-fifty split."

"Oh!" Elwyn's eyes widened. "Fill me in."

"I reckon it's a saleable product. Could fetch a good price."

"Who'd buy it?"

"Off the top of my head, Drayton Manor Park in Tamworth could be interested. If not, there's other sources, specialist maritime species zoos. I'll have to check them out. But I reckon Drayton is the best bet. We'll see."

"I don't want any publicity as I've already said."

"I'll see to that. I'll claim to have caught it myself. After all, I helped you haul it in."

"Fair enough," the fisherman gave a laugh. "It's your baby from now on, Ade, and I'll flatly deny any involvement. I've got an old crate back home that the crab will just about go in."

"And the sooner I hit the road for home, the better."

Adrian regarded their capture with a kind of fondness. It might just turn out to be a money spinner.

* * *

"What the hell have you got there?" Adrian's attractive, dark haired, petite partner, Alison Evans, hugged a coat around her shoulders and came across to the edge of the big pool where the Discovery was backed up. Her torchlight focused on the wooden crate which he was attempting to drag out of the vehicle. "I wasn't expecting you back until tomorrow."

"Something rather important came my way unexpectedly today," he grunted. "Now, if I can just tip this crate out onto the bank …"

"What's inside it?"

"You'll see."

The crate balanced precariously then fell to the ground with a crash of splitting laths.

"Now if you can just give me a hand to tip it up …"

The top flew open with the weight of its captive and the crab rolled down the bank. A tentacle waved and the beam of the torch reflected a flickering of sheer malevolence in the tiny eyes before it hit the water with a mighty splash.

"Ugh!" Alison stepped back. "It's horrible."

"It's our nest egg," he laughed.

"It looks like some kind of crab but it's too big to be one."

"Crab it is and only a baby," he laughed his relief aloud. At least the crustacean was still alive. It had survived the journey and now it was safely in the pool. Step one had been successfully achieved.

"Let's go indoors," he slammed the Discovery door shut, "and I'll explain. Not a word to a soul, though. Right now it's our secret, the biggest we've ever had."

Fred, the retired Hilton farmer, had tossed and squirmed restlessly since coming up to bed a couple of hours earlier. Indigestion always followed his eating pork pie. Right now he vowed never to touch it again as he had resolved many times before, a resolution which was always broken. It was irresistible, especially at supper time.

"For God's sake!" his wife, Pat, glanced again at the dial of the radio alarm on the bedside table. "It's nearly two o'clock and I haven't had a wink of sleep with you flaying about. I'll make damn sure I don't buy any more pork pies. You'll never learn."

"Sorry love. I'll give 'em up, I promise."

"I've heard that before."

"Shush!" He held up a finger. "I can hear something in the garden. Sounds like it could be a fox." He threw back the duvet, slid out of bed.

"Where are you going now?"

"I'll get the gun and the big torch."

"Oh, for God's sake, what next? It isn't as though we even keep poultry these days."

Fred ignored her. His keys rattled in the door of the steel gun cabinet. He lifted out his Miroku 12-bore over-and-under and groped on the small shelf above until he located a couple of cartridges, ex-Home Guard loads with a single lead ball, reserved for such occasions as this. They would do the trick, all right.

Slowly, carefully, he opened the bedroom window. With the shotgun at his shoulder, he flicked on the torch with his left hand, sent a powerful beam across the lawn towards the shrubbery at the top.

Amidst the foliage he glimpsed something reddish-brown which moved. A fox, undoubtedly. His forefinger squeezed the trigger and a deafening crash shattered the stillness of the winter night. His target disappeared from view.

"Got im!" He shouted.

"And woken up the entire neighbourhood in the bargain," Pat groaned. "Now, please come back to bed and let's get some sleep."

"All right," he put his gun away. "I'll go check that fox in the morning. He'll be lying dead in the shrubbery, I know."

* * *

Pat was stirring her husband's porridge on the stove when he came back indoors from the garden.

"Well?" She did not turn around. "I presume there's a fox lying dead in the shrubbery. At least then waking everybody up in Hilton might have been worth it!"

"I don't understand it," there was a puzzled expression on Fred's features. "For a start, take a look out of the window."

She turned, stared across the lawn. "My goodness, it looks like you've run the rotavator across it! What the dickens has made all of those ruts?"

"I dunno," he shook his head. "At first glance I thought we'd had a wild boar digging it up. Remember that paddock we saw down by the Forest of Dean last year, all chewed up in a single night by boars?"

"There aren't any wild boar in this part of the country."

"Exactly. So we can rule them out."

"What then?"

"It hasn't been done by moles or foxes. All I can think of is badgers digging for worms. This is rather odd, though."

He held out his hand, displayed a jagged triangle of a brownish colour nestling in his palm.

"Whatever's that, Fred?"

"It's a piece of crab shell. I should know, I've seen enough crabs when I've been fishing down in Dorset."

"Then what's it doing in our garden?"

"I can only presume that I missed that fox last night but it was carrying the remains of a crab which it had scavenged from somewhere. When I fired and missed, it dropped this piece of shell and ran."

"I guess that sounds feasible. Now, come and get your breakfast and let's hope we have a more peaceful night tonight, no more foxes in the garden and certainly no more pork pie for supper!"

Daylight seemed to take an eternity to arrive. Adrian sat at the kitchen table sipping a mug of strong tea. He could have gone to the pool with his powerful foxing lamp but decided against it. The last thing he wanted was to alarm the crustacean, all he needed was a glimpse to satisfy himself that it was still there, still alive. He would have to think about feeding it, that might be a problem. Eels were his first choice, that fishmonger in Lichfield usually stocked them but the problem was quantity.

The stair door opened and Alison appeared, fully dressed. That was unusual as she mostly remained in her dressing gown until after breakfast.

"Up bright and early, I see," he greeted her.

"I'm coming out to the pool with you," she answered.

"Whatever for? I'm only going for a quick looksee, make sure …"

"I don't want you going alone, Ade. What I saw of that crab last night scares me. It looked a nasty bit of work. A nip from an ordinary crab can be painful but those pincers look as though they could do a lot of damage."

"Like I said, we're only going for a peek. If all is well then I'll phone Drayton Manor and see if they're interested. If we can do a deal we could well be rid of Crabby before the day is out."

"I sincerely hope so," she shuddered, poured herself a mug of tea.

"Another ten minutes and it might be light enough to see," he checked the window again. "It seems to be getting a little lighter. Damned cold but it's raw and not freezing which is a good thing for our temporary guest. The last thing I need is for him to die, and the sooner we get him into salt water, the better."

Daylight was coming fast as they stepped outside, Adrian in the lead with Alison at his heels. Both of them were apprehensive. In the cold light of a winter morning the whole scheme seemed crazy, like the lingering remnants of a nightmare. A huge baby crab, spawned by an outsize ravenous beast from four decades ago, now lying on a quiet Midlands smallholding.

Adrian's step slowed, he found himself creeping up onto the high bank. Would the crustacean still be here? Would it be alive or dead?

"There's no sign of it," his voice was a whisper as he scanned the surface of the water.

"Perhaps it's resting on the bottom," Alison replied. "Or it's died."

Then his gaze focused on the far bank.

"What the hell's happened over there?"

"Looks like somebody's been digging out the bank," Alison clutched her husband's arm.

"Let's take a closer look," he quickened his step, circuited the water's edge.

Something most certainly had been disturbing the soil which he had recently excavated to make a bank surrounding the pool. Deep incisions which had created mini avalanches down into the water.

"Maybe a badger of a fox," Alison offered a lame explanation. She avoided blaming their recent overnight resident for the unsightly diggings.

"No way," Adrian knelt and examined the ground. "Look how the soil has been ripped away, not digging but … but as though something was struggling to obtain a hold on a near vertical surface."

His gaze turned in the opposite direction. "Jesus Christ, it's gone across the allotment area, heading for the fields beyond!"

"The crab!" She stated the obvious.

"Yeah," he groaned. "It's escaped, headed for Christ knows where. Hilton for a start."

"What are we going to do, Ade?"

"I don't know," he took a deep breath and she was aware how his hand trembled like her own. "Frankly, there's nothing we can do right now. We don't know how long it's been gone and how far it can travel. Seems it didn't think much of our pool so it's gone looking for somewhere else."

"Hadn't we better report it?"

"Shit, no, that's the last thing we need to do. There's a law against keeping dangerous wild animals without a licence and secure enclosures. I don't know whether giant crabs fall into that category but you can bet your life if it causes any damage or attacks anybody they'd throw the book at us."

"Oh, my God!"

"Don't worry, love," he squeezed her hand. "Nobody knows I brought it back here except old Elwyn Jones and he won't say anything for sure. So we keep mum, deny all knowledge of it, not that anybody's likely to ask us. All we can do is keep our ears open and see if there are any reports of a crab on the loose. Frankly, now I'm hoping that it just dies in some secluded place and nobody finds it."

"Which reminds me," she said. "I thought I heard a shot in the night, seemed to come from somewhere down by the Ellett farm."

"Probably somebody out lamping for foxes," he shrugged his shoulders. "Come on, let's go and have some breakfast then I've got work to do. First job will be to repair that bank, just in case anybody should come nosing around and figures out what's happened."

4

Festive week saw an influx of visitors to Lichfield in spite of the cold weather. Most people had an extended Christmas break and needed something to occupy their days. A major tourist attraction, there were places to visit such as the cathedral and Doctor Johnson's birthplace. Cafés and restaurants were open, anticipating lively trade.

Then there was the historic Minster Pool below the cathedral, dating back hundreds of years and re-styled by the poet Ann Seward in an attempt to replicate London's Serpentine.

New and higher railings had been erected on the walkway alongside, a contentious issue with some older residents, primarily for the safety of young children. That did not prevent a regular depositing of litter in the water, though, along with shopping trolleys from nearby supermarkets.

A small crowd thronged the path alongside the pool. Usually there was a flock of waterfowl to be seen, Canada geese, mallard, moorhens and coots.

Today the water was devoid of any species of wildlife even though the surface was unfrozen. That was strange indeed.

Trevor Brown was a burly man with his wife and children trailing behind him. He wore a t-shirt beneath an open jacket, a demonstration of his intended macho image. His loud, booming voice remarked upon the absence of waterfowl.

"Where have all the bloody geese and ducks gone?" He announced for the benefit of other tourists. "Waste o' time bringin' a bag of bread with you." He skimmed a couple of slices across the pool. "The buggers can't eat bleedin' polystyrene chip trays. No wonder they've all pissed off."

"Daddy," one of his small daughters interrupted his coarse commentary, "those railings up there are broken."

"By vandals who chuck all this rubbish in, no doubt," he moved along to inspect the damage, a section of iron railings twisted into a tangle. "Must've been a strong bloke who did that. Youths today are usually wimps."

"Daddy!"

"What now?" Bloody kids never stop chattering.

"There's a crab down there. It's huge!"

"Rubbish!" All the same he moved in for a closer look then stared in disbelief. "Bloody hell, she's right. Just come and look at this, Marion. A crab the size of a bleedin' dog!"

As his wife approached for a closer look, nearby tourists moved closer.

"It's impossible," somebody commented. "Must be a model, somebody playing a joke."

As if it heard, the crab in the shallow water moved, lifted a pincer. There were gasps of amazement all round.

"I don't like the look of that bugger," Trevor Brown announced. "I'm going to call the cops." He fumbled in his pocket, found his mobile, pressed a trio of 9s with a thick thumb."

"Which emergency service do you require?"

"Police. And make it snappy."

"What is the reason for your call, sir?"

"There's a crab as big as a bloody dog in Minster Pool, Lichfield."

Seconds of silence followed, then "Did you say a large crab, sir?"

"I bloody well did, and it don't look very friendly. There's kids around."

"Should there be a crab in the pool then it is not an emergency and certainly not a police matter. I must warn you that hoax calls are liable to prosecution. However, I am treating this as a bad joke on your part and if you take my advice you will not call again."

The line went dead.

The gathering of listeners had backed off. A couple had walked away. Nobody wanted to be involved.

"Then I'll ring the bleedin' council," the big man's features were red. "They're bound to have somebody on emergency callout."

"A crab you say," the official at the other end of the line had been contacted after a wait of several minutes. "I can assure you that there are no crabs in Minster Pool."

"I tell you there bloody well is!" A sudden idea that might spark a reaction. "And a section of the railings has been broken down. And there are kids playing around it."

"We'll get somebody down there as soon as possible."

Well, that one had worked! The caller moved back to a bench and sat down, his wife and family following suit. Suddenly it did not seem so cold.

Those who had clustered around him had dispersed.

It was over an hour before two council officials arrived. The senior officer viewed the twisted railings with an impassive expression on his angular features. His younger companion wore overalls and carried a roll of orange netting obviously to secure the open gap on a temporary basis.

"Vandals," the former announced. "Probably the ones who threw that shopping trolley into the water."

"Bugger the vandals," came the response from the man on the bench. "What about that crab down there?" He pointed towards the shallows below the bank. "What d'you make of that, then?"

The council men moved over to the twisted ironwork, peered down into the water. Both shook their heads, looked at each other with raised eyebrows.

"There's no crab down there."

"Because it's probably moved off into deeper water. I tell you we all saw it."

There was no response. Between them the two men unrolled the plastic netting and began fixing it over the open space.

"Let's bloody leave 'em to stew!" Trevor Brown rose to his feet, motioned to his family to follow him through the gap in the wall behind to the adjacent Minster car park. "We've wasted the best part of two hours."

When he reached his car he discovered a parking penalty ticket tucked under the windscreen wiper. The traffic wardens, like the crab in the pool, had been and gone.

5

Jake usually managed to 'pick up a bird' at one of the city's clubs. There were always plenty from which to choose, those who came 'dolled up to the eyeballs' and looking for a one-night stand.

In his early twenties and reasonably good looking, he eyed them up before moving in. Tonight he had moved in on a petite, peroxide blonde plastered with a thick layer of make-up. She watched his approach with dilated pupils.

They danced close and she wasn't slow in making her intentions known. She slid her hands down to his buttocks and pulled him in close, checking for signs of interest and was not disappointed. She looked into his eyes and smiled coyly, Jake knew it was game on.

When they left the club they strolled alongside Minster Pool, hand-in-hand.

"Looks like somebody's wrecked the railings," he remarked "and the council's botched-up temporary repair hasn't lasted long."

The orange plastic netting was strewn across the walkway, pulled clear of the gap in the ironwork.

"You got a place to go to?" She shivered beneath her coat.

"Naw, I live with my folks, can't go back there. You?"

"I share a bedsit with a mate and I'm pretty sure that she'll already be hard at it with some bloke she picked up tonight."

"Shit!"

"It's too bloody cold out here tonight. Where then?"

He leant against the railings and pulled her to him, she felt his erection. Giggling she moved her hand down to it and began rubbing it through his faded jeans. He guided her fingers to the zip and she needed no further invitation to slide it down and grope inside.

Jake felt the cold air on his member. God, I'm not just going to settle for a wank.

"We could go down by the bridge," he suggested. "It'll be more sheltered there."

She did not reply, enjoying the tease of building his arousal.

Something clicked in the darkness behind them.

"What's that noise?" She stiffened, peered on to the lawn area behind her.

Click – click.

"I heard something, a kind of clicking sound." She stopped rubbing him.

"Let's get down to the bridge. We can get through that gap in the fence and …"

A heavy shape, indiscernible in the darkness, launched itself upon them without warning amidst a frantic clicking. The girl screamed, clutching at Jake for support. Something cut her leg deep, like a chainsaw blade slicing its way through to get to her companion. A razor-sharp pincer.

The element of surprise had given the attacker the advantage, knocking them down and pinning them to the ground, it slashed frenziedly with its claws. Clothing was ripped, flesh bared. Screams of fear and pain filled the bitter cold night air. Now the crab was going crazy, human meat was a delicacy which it had not tasted before, far superior to eels and small marine life. Stuffing dripping lengths into its mouth, slurping and dribbling blood.

Soon its victims were silent, mercifully beyond further pain. It fed until it was satisfied and then crouched there as though debating its next move. This was a confusing new world.

Like the trout pool from which it had escaped this stretch of water was also too small for a creature that had once roamed the ocean bed. Some inexplicable sense told it that there was larger water somewhere in the vicinity. It had to find it.

It shifted from its sedentary position and began to shamble away along the tarmac walkway. Its clicking reverberated in the still night air but there was nobody around to hear it.

* * *

The mutilated remains of Jake and his pick-up were discovered by a dog walker early on the following morning. The police arrived within fifteen minutes of the alarm being raised. An ambulance arrived shortly after along with forensics. Minster Pool was cordoned off at both the Dam Street and Bird Street entrances as well as the adjacent car park.

"Looks to me like the work of a crazed dog," Detective Inspector Roughton made an early, uninformed diagnosis.

"No way," the forensics officer looked up from examining the remains of the corpses. "That's what did it, it was underneath the girl."

Roughton stared at the object which the other held up. "What the hell is it?"

"A tiny fragment of crab shell unless I miss my guess. We'll confirm it later."

"Hell's bells! An officer contacted us from HQ yesterday about a hoax call. Some guy claimed to have seen an oversize crab in the pool. He only phoned through because the apparent nutter reported that the railings had been damaged and kids were at risk. My God, we'd better get the pool searched." He gave orders on his radio.

A punt used for retrieving litter was launched within the hour, the boatman using a long handled type of rake to scrape through the depths. Police officers watched from the bank. A systematic search of the entire pool took the best part of two hours at the end of which the craft was pulled back up on to dry land.

"Nothing?" Roughton was still sceptical.

"Nope," the boatman shook his head. "I can guarantee that there's no crab in there."

"Sir!" A sudden interruption came from an officer who had been diligently examining the length of the tarmac walkway. "There's some blood drops up the far end by the Dam Street entrance."

"I'll send for the dog tracker." Roughton used his radio again.

The summoned officer arrived within twenty minutes, a pair of Springer spaniels were given a sniff of the fragment of shell and the bloodstains. They embarked eagerly upon a scent, heading up towards the cathedral. Then they appeared to lose it, doubtless because a road sweeping team had been out early clearing the previous day's litter which included discarded food scraps, pizzas and chips. Some well-meaning resident had washed off the pavement in front of his and neighbouring premises using a strong solution of Dettol.

An initial post mortem of both corpses confirmed that death had occurred at the claws of a creature believed to be a crustacean. An inquest would follow but for the moment the police had no other option than to presume that a crab of immense size was the killer and was still at large.

"Crazy!" Roughton sat at his desk, his head in his hands, addressing a team of detectives. "Evidence shows that we have a giant crab capable of killing humans within the city limits. We don't have the manpower to search every expanse of open water. So we have no option but to wait and see. We can only pray that away from salt water it will simply die. It could well have headed for the nearest river and in due course find its way back to sea. The mystery may never be solved, nor how it came to be here."

Deep down, though, he had a feeling that there would be more deaths. He did not voice his thoughts. The Press were already doing that.

6

Joe Spooner termed himself a 'knight of the road' and in his own way took pride in being an old-fashioned tramp. In his early sixties, he had forgotten his exact age, he had been homeless for the past five years. Unemployed and receiving benefit he had spent virtually all of his allowance on alcohol. In recent years, with no income, he had taken to drinking meths. Unable to pay rent for the house in which he had lived, he had been evicted.

His long hair and beard were white and unkempt. A clutch of blackheads covered the exposed areas of his face, his fingernails were jagged and black with dirt. Two layers of unwashed underwear and some top garments stolen from a clothing bank on the car park kept him reasonably warm.

He had long given up dossing on the streets. He was a loner who objected to sharing sparse shelter with others. Those damned young layabouts ragged him, told him he stank. Maybe he did, so what?

Tonight he found his way down to Stowe Pool. He had planned to sleep down by the Minster bridge but there was a lot of police activity there. Something must have happened, maybe a child had drowned. He really wasn't interested and certainly wasn't going to ask anybody. He kept well clear of the police at all times. Several times he had been stopped in the street and questioned. They had never searched him, though, because no self-respecting copper would touch him. That was another good reason for his abstention from washing. Dirt and grime helped in keeping both the cold and nosey bobbies at bay.

Earlier that day he had sat on the pavement opposite the Market Square, his filthy, tattered upturned cap by his side.

Most passers-by turned their heads away and walked swiftly past. Bastards! Others deliberately gave him a wide berth. One haughty woman even lifted her head and pinched her nose. Bitch! A few tossed coins into his headgear, mostly of small denominations. Stingy fuckers!

All the same, after three hours he had accumulated just over a fiver. It would help. There was a bakery nearby that incorporated a café and ready-made sandwiches. Struggling up on to his feet he stumbled his way to it.

The staff were only too familiar with Joe Spooner but at least they served him, albeit with disdain, not like the supermarkets where officious supervisors had ordered him out on more than one occasion.

He pushed open the door. There was a queue at the counter which instantly moved as far away from him as was possible without losing their places. Two women who were serving exchanged disapproving glances. Joe in the shop was not good for trade. A woman about to enter from the street changed her mind and turned away. Please your bleedin' self, missus!

"Can I help you?" One of the assistants asked but it was clear from her expression that she would rather not serve him.

Joe knew only too well what he could buy for a fiver; the previous day's loaves were on offer at half price. He stocked up, scrounged a carrier bag. Pairs of eyes followed him out of the door. Somebody announced 'phew, what a stink!'

Now it was time to find somewhere to hole up for the night. With Minster Pool no longer an option it had to be neighbouring Stowe. There was a boathouse on the nearside adjoining a narrow beach below the high bank. He had a square of canvas tarpaulin which he carried rolled up. Beneath it, if it came on to rain, he would be perfectly dry.

His shabby coat and layers of grubby underwear were as good as a blanket.

As dusk approached Joe made himself ready for the coming night. Jutting out from the shore was a raised base with an entrance on the lake for the purpose of accommodating a boat. The dry landside of this offered shelter from the worst of the elements, the high bank at the rear acting as a windbreak.

He ate some of the bread, there was enough left for breakfast the following morning. After that, tomorrow was another day, as the old saying went.

Darkness closed in. So peaceful, just the sound of the water lapping the shore a few yards below him. Soothing. He dozed.

Some time later a noise awoke him. Normally he would have slept through it except that it was an unfamiliar sound, not that of late night revellers on the path which circuited the pool, nor contented quacking of mallard out on the water. Something strange, a kind of … clicking.

He lay there wondering what it could be. Maybe items of floating litter knocking together or the beaks of wildfowl as they fed. No, that wasn't right.

Click-click-clickety-click. Nearer and louder, just a few yards off shore. He wished that he had a torch but his finances did not run to such luxuries. He eased up on to his elbows, peered, strained his eyes in the enshrouding darkness.

Something was coming up out of the water, a shape which he could not define except that it was about the size of a big dog. Scratching on the stones, clicking, waving limbs that might have been legs.

Glowing pinpoints were reflected from the street lighting from the housing estate behind. Those were surely tiny eyes. He did not like the look of them.

Jesus, what the hell was it?

Joe fumbled in his coat pocket, found a box of matches. Some of the contents spilled out as he scrabbled in it. He struck the brimstone head on the sandpaper, it flared briefly before the night breeze extinguished it but its small glare lit up the sheer horror of the creature which was now within a yard of him.

A monster crab clicked with every inch of its approach.

Slowly Joe Spooner got to his feet, his creaking, aged limbs responding to the terror which gripped him. He threw the tarpaulin at his adversary; it dropped over the crab but was thrust aside and the advance was barely halted.

Stumbling in his clumsy flight he made it to the bank, clutched at the top in an attempt to pull himself up. Tussocks of grass were uprooted in his gnarled hands and he toppled backwards, hit the crab as he fell.

It had him in an instant, vicious pincers closing over a kicking leg. Bone crunched, the amputation was instant. The severed leg was thrust aside, now an arm was gripped.

Joe gave a throaty scream as he lost another limb. Now it had him pinned down and his filthy garb was ripped away, a pincer digging deep into his scrawny frame in search of intestine delicacies first before meat was torn from bones.

Chomping, squelching, the crab had not eaten since it had devoured the young couple by Minster Pool. Tender or scrawny stringy flesh, it made no difference as it ate with relish, using its claws to rip the carcass apart in search of more.

Finally all that remained of the tramp were severed limbs and a head, the latter cast aside yet propped upright, wide dead eyes seeming to stare at its bloody remains.

Only then did the crab head back into the water with an almost casual shamble. Gone was the frantic fever of hunger. It was satisfied and now it would rest. Until its next meal.

7

Miss Rathmore, a staid retired sister from the Victoria Hospital, still rose at 6.30 just as she had done throughout her working life. First job of the day, after a cup of tea, was to walk her terrier, Flip.

This morning her daily constitutional would have to be around Stowe Pool for Minster was closed to the public. She had read about the awful happening there. The presence of a giant crab stretched the imagination to its limits. It was the sort of rubbish that sold newspapers. She felt a little twinge of guilt at buying one but convinced herself that she had only purchased it in order to keep abreast of the forthcoming General Election news.

Dawn had broken, a grey misty start to the day, as she started along the path that circled the pool, heading in a clockwise direction which would terminate by the boathouse.

Flip seemed strangely subdued this morning, following close at her heels instead of dashing up and down the banks and splashing in the edge of the water as he usually did. She hoped he was all right. If not, she would take him to the vet later.

Past St. Chad's church at the far end and now heading in a westward direction she saw the outline of the boathouse looming up ahead. Another ten minutes and she would be back home, cosy and warm for the rest of the day. She didn't begrudge Flip his daily walks but at this time of the year they could be somewhat arduous.

Flip decided to run on ahead as far as the boathouse. Then he stopped, his posture somewhat cowed. He made no attempt to run down the bank as he usually did. A low growl came from his throat, fear rather than aggression, the way he often behaved when he spied another dog.

"What on earth's the matter with you, my darling?" She increased her step, holding his lead at the ready. The sooner he was back on the leash the better.

Now the hackles on his neck were standing upright. Clearly something was disturbing him but there was nothing in sight which might have caused him to behave in this manner. He advanced to the top of the bank, drew back. It was something down below which was responsible for his behaviour.

She reached him, clipped the lead on his collar and then peered over into the water gently lapping the stony beach. Flip was pulling back, whining.

"Stop it!" She croaked. "Let me see what ... oh, my goodness, I ... whatever is it?"

The object that she stared at below the surface of the water bobbed up into full view. It was a human arm, torn and bloodied, some fingers missing from the hand.

Miss Rathmore gave a wheezing gasp of horror. Flip jerked on his leash, almost pulling her over. Even as she stared an equally mauled and bloody leg floated into view. And there was something else a few yards further out. She did not want to see it but it swirled as though deliberately showing itself to her. Look!

It was the ravaged remnants of a body, stomach ripped asunder, head missing, just the ragged stump of the neck remaining.

The terrier pulled with all of its strength, almost toppling its mistress. Miraculously she kept her footing. Flip was panicking, tugging for home. She followed at an unsteady gait.

Ten minutes later she was back in her hallway, the front door locked just in case … Somehow her shaking, bony finger managed to dial 999.

* * *

"That bloody crab's in Stowe Pool!" Detective-Inspector Roughton shouted through the open doorway of his office to Sergeant Wilkins. "And there's another body by the boathouse. Tell forensics, and we'll need the armed support unit, too. Let's go!"

Police, the forensics officer, an ambulance and three armed support officers in riot gear congregated at the scene. The boatman was on his way. This time they would put paid to this elusive crustacean, Roughton promised. He no longer doubted its presence within the city limits.

The sizeable rowing boat was launched, a long handled grapnel lying across its bows. Only a few weeks earlier it had been used to retrieve the body of a suicide.

The trio of officers loaded their Heckler & Koch MP5 9mm sub-machine guns. These weapons had a magazine capacity of 30 rounds so 90 shots in rapid succession were ready for the killer crab. It could not possibly survive such a hail of bullets.

The boatman took the oars, began to row across the width of the pool. His duffle coat was fastened up to his neck, his hood pulled well down, just unshaven features of indeterminable age peeping from within. He had been called from his bed on his day off and was far from happy. The thought of meeting up with whatever had dismembered and gorged on that couple by the Minster, and now this latest victim, was not a pleasant prospect. He consoled himself with the thought that these cops would shoot on sight.

Rowing, stopping, probing the depths with the grapnel. Nothing.

"I reckon we're wasting our time," he called out over his shoulder to his companions.

"Keep going. We'll tell you when to stop."

An hour dragged by and then came a shout from one of the policemen. "There's something up there at the far end. Now it's ducked down again."

All eyes were on the distant shoreline as the boat pushed forward. Weapons were held at the ready.

"It was definitely something," the officer who had raised the alarm tried to sound confident. If it was found to be some inanimate item of rubbish then the ribbing would go on for weeks.

"There it is!"

Fifty yards ahead an ungainly shape was emerging from the shallows on to the stony stretch below the bank. There was no doubt in the minds of the observers that this was the elusive crustacean, finally flushed from its temporary watery lair.

"Don't shoot," the officer in command shouted, "we could ricochet the church and houses. Faster, boatman!"

The oars were worked at full speed, the boat shot forward.

"Blast, it's climbing up the bank."

"It'll be easier to shoot on dry land."

The pursuers had underestimated the agility and speed of their quarry. The overhanging bank presented no obstacle to the fleeing crab. It crossed the shingled path, descended the opposite side and headed across the tarmac road.

An oncoming car braked, swerved, missed it by inches and skidded. The driver stared into his rear view mirror in disbelief, pulled into the kerb. Seconds later armed police were pulling open the driver's door.

"Have you seen a crab, mate?"

"Bloody hell, yes!"

"Which way did it go?"

He checked his mirror again. The road behind was empty.

"I dunno."

The officers broke into a run, fanned out across the road, weapons at the ready. Houses, driveways, gardens, an adjoining road. They pulled up breathless.

"It could've gone anywhere," the officer in charge groaned. "I'll send for backup, the dog-handler. It can't get far."

* * *

The shambling crab covered distance at a rate which belied its shape and size. Eventually it came to farmland, fields, hedgerows and ditches which afforded it cover in its flight. Yet its instinct told it that it needed a more secure refuge, if only temporarily. Preferably a large expanse of water but, failing that, thick undergrowth where it could bury itself until the hunt for it had died down.

Only then would it try to find its way back to the coast.

8

Alex Kahn had opted out of University at the end of his second year. He had informed both the authorities and his parents that he was only taking a year out at the end of which he would return. That saved a lot of hassle and pressure being put upon him to change his mind. Of course, he wouldn't be going back. Certainly not now.

He had been educated at the Cathedral School where he had excelled himself academically but his most bitter disappointment was in being rejected for the choir. Mr Norton, the choir master, had an unfounded dislike for him which was the only reason, Alex was sure, that he had not become a chorister. From that day onward he had become an embittered loner and, even at uni, was determined to take his revenge on, not just Norton but the school itself. Withers, the headmaster, had also gone out of his way to make life unpleasant for him.

"I'm taking a year out of uni," he informed his parents with a sullen expression on his face and defiance in his tone.

"What!" his father shouted. "Don't be a fool. You're well on the way to becoming an expert in technology. You might even get a job in government security, like GCHQ."

"I'm opting out," Alex replied stubbornly.

"Then you're not going to lodge here."

"Please, both of you ..." His mother began.

"Shut up!" Her husband silenced her.

So Alex left home, found himself a cheap bedsit and claimed benefit. Now he had time to plan his vengeance and resorted to using the internet, which was where he come into contact with Jahn.

Jahn gave him access to the 'dark web.' Bomb making was explained in detail, complicated but not beyond Alex's technical talents. His excitement grew.

Quite by chance, on a ramble through the countryside, he came upon an old wartime explosives dump. A sizeable reinforced underground place which resembled many of these shelters built during the Second World War, it was hidden in. an area of unmanaged woodland, its exterior covered by thick brambles. He might have ignored it except for some brick steps going down through the undergrowth. Curiosity overcame him and the following day he returned with a borrowed pair of shears. It took him over an hour to chop away the obstructing briars, his scratches going unheeded, until eventually he came upon a rotted wooden door. A rusted padlock secured it but it only needed a strong kick to expose the entrance to a dark and musty smelling interior.

His torch beam revealed work benches, empty steel containers and shelving. Seventy years ago, when peace had returned to Britain, the small workforce had no further need for this place. They had left, securing the door behind them, and clearly nobody had been here since. If the owner of this woodland was aware of its existence, he had simply left it to decay beneath the dense vegetation.

Alex's thoughts returned to his study of bomb making. His bedsit was no place to work on explosives and their technical involvement. Here was a place where he would be uninterrupted, where he could store everything he required.

By night he stole the fertilizer he required from a local farm. It was easy, it would not even be missed. The access to the resources that Jahn had provided gave him all the information he needed on equipment required and how to obtain it. He was careful not to draw attention to himself and not leave any electronic trace.

Slowly, a small explosives factory was installed in that former WD bomb store.

He decided to make three bombs and had already determined their locations. The school, obviously; and the cathedral, they had denied him a place in the choir and afterwards they would not have a choir at all! He deliberated over the third, it was Jahn who suggested Doctor Johnson's birthplace in the Market Square. This would hit the city's tourist trade making it look like a terrorist attack rather than just an act of revenge on the school.

They had to be synchronized explosions, the trio all going off at the same time. The most complicated aspect of bomb making was getting the timing device right. It was fairly simple just for a single explosive but three presented a huge challenge. The internet instructions were somewhat vague on this, no more than a brief reference.

He sought Jahn's advice.

"Set them separately and then install the connector", Jahn was somewhat vague in just how this could be achieved. Alex suspected that the other did not really know the intricate details.

"I will check out the procedure."

He didn't come back to Alex on this.

Alex had other plans to finalise. On the day in question he would set up the timing device and then make a hasty departure from the city. By train to London, then on to Heathrow. He had an airline ticket booked for Turkey, a return so it looked as if he was coming back. He had relatives in that country which made everything sound plausible. He wouldn't be visiting them. Once in Turkey he would head for the Syrian border. Jahn had instructed him where to go, a contact would meet him there.

All the same he was nervous.

* * *

The three bombs were completed, he stood back and admired his handiwork. All he had to do now was to place them in his chosen targets and install the timer in readiness.

His mouth went dry.

Inside the cathedral there were vergers on duty, walking around and watching visitors. He dropped a coin into the offertory box, made sure it clinked loudly. Reconnaissance was slow, standing and admiring stained glass windows.

He slid into a pew, knelt in mock prayer. Searching for a secluded place where nobody else was likely to look.

Some form of restoration work was in progress around the chapter house vestibule. Workmen had piled their tools alongside a small pile of rubble waiting to be cleared. There was no sign of these men, they probably would not be recommencing their labours until after festive week.

He checked that nobody was around. There did not appear to be a CCTV camera in the immediate vicinity. As a precaution he dropped a coin, bent down to retrieve it and in one deft movement slid his device beneath a pile of broken slabs.

He straightened up, let out an audible sigh of relief. He was sweating profusely. Then he continued his stroll down the main aisle, admiring more stained glass windows and the magnificent architecture, as he went.

A verger nodded to him. Then, outside, he quickened his step and headed back to the bedsit.

* * *

Placing a bomb in the school had to be a night time task, one that would be much more nerve racking. Like burgling. His fear was that the gates of this former bishop's palace would be closed and locked. They were shut but not padlocked, either an oversight or routine. He eased through, closed them after him, carefully ensuring that they did not clang.

He checked his watch. 11.30pm. No lights showed apart from a couple shining from upper windows. He used the shrubbery for his approach, slipped on a balaclava, just in case CCTV picked him up. He would remove it before entering the building, a precaution should he encounter anybody.

Providing an excuse for his presence at this hour would be tricky. Pupils would be on holiday, just a few members of staff remaining. He hoped that both Norton and Withers would be around when the bomb detonated. The fuckers would get their due deserts then!

The main door creaked as he pushed it open. He remained on the step, ears tuned in case there were approaching footsteps. There were none. Distant and muffled he heard voices, a conversation. All was well. So far.

The library was his destination and he found it easily enough. It was in darkness so he used his torch, just a quick flash of its beam on the floor to ceiling shelves. In those few seconds it focused on a sizeable volume, the gilt lettering on the spine glinting – 'The Life of Samuel Johnson LL.D' How appropriate, he grinned to himself.

Now, working by feel in the pitch blackness, he pulled the heavy tome forward. The gap behind it was ideal for his purpose and he slid the bomb into place, pushed the book back as far as it would go.

Job done. His departure was swift and encountered no problems. A couple of minutes later he was in the Close and heading back to his bedsit. Just one more explosive device to plant tomorrow. Doctor Johnson's birthplace would have to be a daytime visit, mingling with the visitors in that abode. In some respects it would be easier, just a matter of sleight of hand when nobody was looking. One final thought again brought a frown to his face. He needed to check the timing device in the bunker, consult the internet again and maybe Jahn too.

The worst scenario would be if none of the trio of bombs detonated due to his bungling the technology. There would be no opportunity to go and check them. He would have played his last cards. The bomb disposal squad would render them harmless and doubtless there would be some evidence that would lead the police to him.

The sooner tomorrow was over, his targets reduced to rubble and he was on his way to Turkey, the better.

9

The following day he was back in the bunker, his laptop on the dusty bench beside the timing device. Jahn still hadn't got back to him. He continued to research every site he could find on bomb making. All singles, mostly on operating car bombs. There was no mention of synchronizing multi-explosions.

He experimented with numerous settings; each time his efforts were rejected. He was becoming increasingly frustrated. He knew it was possible, it was just a question of working it out.

Hours passed. Outside darkness had closed in. His small lamp was dimming, the batteries were running low. He should have bought some replacements, an oversight but it was too late now. Somehow he had to solve his problem, it would be too risky to leave it another day. Sod's law somebody would discover one of his bombs on the morrow.

Fatigue and desperation were overtaking him. He re-visited a site Jahn had previously mentioned, found a link. Reading as fast as he could before he lost his useable light, he finally found the answer, a way to link the trio to the digital clock on the device. Previously it had cut out. Now it held. He gave a long sigh of relief.

And that was when he heard a noise outside, somewhere up above in the dense undergrowth, a scratching sound. Panic froze him for a moment. He was so close to completing his task. Surely not, he'd been so careful not to be discovered.

Alex tensed, the noise began again.

Click-click. Like somebody was using a pair of shears on the briars. No, it wasn't quite right. What the hell was it?

Some nocturnal creature, badger or fox, its claws scratching on stones?

Now a scraping. Whatever it was it was descending those broken brick steps down to the entrance, dislodging fragments as it come.

Click-click-clickety-click.

Woodwork cracked, the remnants of the old door disintegrating further. A loud crash. Now, whatever it was, was in the doorway.

Alex grabbed his torch, sent a shaky, dull beam in the direction of the doorway. That was when the intruder was revealed to him in its full, inexplicable awfulness. He let out a strangled scream which died away in his throat.

It was a huge crab, the same size as that of the Doberman which his parents kept at home!

It was impossible, a figment of his imagination brought on by his exhaustion and frustration. Yet the torch beam reflected on tiny eyes that glowed like embers in a dying fire, glinted at him with sheer malevolence, flickered lust for human flesh and the opportunity to satisfy its gnawing hunger. The tramp by Stowe Pool had long been digested.

Alex backed away until he came up against a stack of empty metal crates. One over balanced and fell to the floor with a resounding crash. If only there had been another exit from this tomb-like place. But there wasn't, the wartime workforce had not needed one.

"Go away!" A useless whisper.

The crab remained immobile, watching, savouring its next feed. Its victim was trapped, it would not be going anywhere. Its limited train of thought still recalled those humans which were hunting it. This one was easy prey.

A pincer had become caught up in a section of smashed door. It freed itself, sending the obstruction clattering across the floor.

Only then did the crustacean move. An ungainly heave of its body brought it inside the underground room where it squatted on the filthy floor. Like Alex, it was exhausted after its long trek on land, so tiring after a life spent on the ocean bed. It rested momentarily to regain its strength.

He shouted in the vain hope that he might frighten it away. His rasping voice echoed in the confined space. The crab did not move, continued to stare at him with its tiny eyes.

He wondered if he could rush past it, a sudden sprint and a leap. Years ago he had won the hurdles event on sports day at school.

The crab eased itself forward. Now maybe three yards separated human and this monster from the deep.

Alex's legs were trembling, threatened to throw him to the floor, but it was now or never. He shone the torch on the other's frightening features, hoped that it would be dazzled.

Then he launched himself into what he prayed was a lightning dash. A leap at first but then his limbs buckled and he sprawled headlong on to the crab, splayed across its shell like a sacrificial victim.

A pincer reacted with unbelievable speed, took a leg and crunched it. Bone cracked and then the amputation was complete. A second leg was seized and suffered the same fate.

Alex screamed in agony, slid to the floor, a legless writhing trunk, arms flaying. Blood sprayed onto the walls.

The crab had an arm now, cut through it and cast it aside. The other followed. Like chicken wings it was not interested in bony limbs, just the stomach which offered a delicious repast.

By this time Alex was unconscious. Death came when his attacker laid him on the floor and ripped deep into his abdomen, slurping on tender flesh and succulent entrails. It fed noisily and greedily, dribbling blood and slimy lungs.

Soon it had devoured every morsel and squatted amidst the human debris when it was satisfied. Not only had it found food but also a hiding place which it was seeking, a safe refuge from its hunters. It would sleep and then resume the search for a route back to the ocean.

Scraping the human body parts aside, it moved its blood splattered body in an attempt to find a more comfortable posture for the remainder of the night.

A raised claw came into contact with the bench behind it. It rocked slightly but the force was not enough to topple it. The crab settled down to rest unaware of the slight whirring sound coming from the bench.

Several hours passed and a shaft of light shone through the shattered doorway to the bunker. The crab stirred not wanting to move but in order to survive it would have to get to the ocean soon. All was still and quiet not even birdsong, just an audible *click-click-click*.

In the early stillness of the cold winter morning it picked over the remains of Alex Khan's mutilated body, deriving what remaining sustenance there was to be had. With nothing left, even Alex's 'chicken wings' picked over, the crab made a move and shambled towards the entrance.

Click-click-click.

It got to the base of the brick steps and hesitated as if gathering strength for the climb. It started the ascent …

The ensuing explosion burst the munitions store asunder, sent its concrete structure high into the dawn sky above the woodland, along with fragments of crab and the bloodied remnants of its final gory repast.

The surrounding trees were torn from their roots and hurled in all directions together with stones and soil. Somewhere in the wood nearby a fire was starting.

Amidst the litter strewn by the explosion, a huge crater remained caused by the bomb destined for the birthplace of Doctor Johnson.

* * *

Detective Inspector Roughton rubbed his tired eyes and stared at the massive crater amidst the fallen trees and debris littering an acre or so of what had once been ancient woodland.

"An unexploded bomb left from the wartime days, I guess," he sighed.

"Hang on, sir," an officer stepped forward, "there's a human body part down there. It looks like a hand."

"Undoubtedly some idiot was messing about down there and detonated it. Doubtless forensics will put the whole story together. Well, there's nothing we can do here. Our job is to find that bloody crab. We'd better head for the next stretch of open water. We're bound to catch up with it sooner or later."

At least he hoped so. This whole business was becoming exceedingly exhausting and was wasting valuable police time.

THE DECOY

Decoying is not guaranteed to work as the hunter intends

Dugan waited until the moon rose before he made his way down to the beach. Tall and lithe, he moved with a stealthy purposefulness, using the shadows to his advantage. "See without being seen" was his motto, whether it was poaching salmon from the riverbank up at Dolgellau or knocking pheasants from their roosts in the game coverts at Staylittle.

Christ, today had been unbelievable, a bizarre nightmare in the scorching summer sun. His ears throbbed from the constant heavy gunfire, the screaming of terror-stricken holidaymakers. The death toll, ran into dozens. He felt the sweat chilling on his body and was unable to suppress a shudder. He had to be bloody crazy coming back down here when at any second those monsters might lurch out of the incoming tide to launch yet another attack.

Crabs as big as cows, lusting for human flesh and blood, shredding the bodies of their victims. Those mighty claws, munching and slurping their prey, seemingly invincible in the hail of gunfire from the heavy artillery which lined the remnants of the wrecked promenade.

Dugan glanced back briefly and saw the flooded Marine Parade with its barricades. Another platoon of soldiers had recently arrived but wouldn't do any good, the military were no more than a token force sent to try and pacify public hysteria.

Sure, the big guns had accounted for the odd crab. Dugan had watched the crustacean corpses being winched onto trucks, transported to some laboratory where the boffins would try to come up with explanations. Did it really matter why the crabs had mutated, suffice to say that they had? And Barmouth was only the start, they would wreck every coastal town in Britain, claiming the shores for their own. Dugan wondered how far inland these creatures could travel, perhaps it was better not to think about it.

You're getting windy, he told himself, stroking the barrels of the heavy gun beneath his arm in an effort to regain some of his former confidence. This was no ordinary shotgun. He held it out, studied its silhouette in the wan moonlight. A double-barrelled sixteen gauge with a 9.3x82R rifle barrel beneath. A 'drilling' made in Germany at the turn of the century, designed so that the pheasant shooters could switch to the rifle if a wild boar suddenly broke cover. Then they could flick the lever across which sprung up the peep site and the rear trigger would fire the heavy bullet. Some of the latter day white hunters had used this weapon effectively against big game. If it was capable of knocking down a charging elephant then it would blow a giant crab to hell, Dugan had decided earlier in the day. Provided you hit it in the right place, got your sights on that evil leering face beneath the armour-plated shell and blasted it right between the eyes. The secret lay in getting your bullet beneath the shell, those soldiers on the harbour had been blazing away from an elevated position and their bullets were deflected harmlessly away. An odd fluke shot split a shell, rolled a crab over, but that was all.

The army had cleared the beaches and declared the shoreline a no-go area around midday. The sightseers, the sensation seeking crowds that thronged the seafront, were their biggest headache. The police had erected barriers in an attempt to keep them back but Dugan knew the cliff paths and had made a detour under cover of darkness that had brought him right down to the battle zone. It was his only chance of shooting one of the crabs, securing a trophy for himself, there was a ready market for crab meat and these big buggers came by the kilo. And the huge shell would fetch a fortune if it was all in one piece. The British Museum maybe, or even abroad. If he worked it right, he was onto a gold mine.

Just one shell that was all he had because the specific ammunition for the rifle part of his gun was not readily available. One shot, there would be no time for a second. If his aim was true, fine. If he missed …

He followed the rocks that led down to the tide, bent low because every few minutes that blinding searchlight beam swung across the beach. The rocks were higher now, the result of an avalanche some years ago that had caused part of the cliffs to spill onto the beach. Here he was hidden from the shore in a world of dark shadows and moonbeam patterns, rock pools draped with seaweed that glinted in the ethereal light. A night-world that watched and waited. Just the gentle lapping of the waves on the shingle, you had to strain your ears to catch the voices of the soldiers in the distance.

It was here that Dugan stumbled on the body. He recoiled and cried out when his bare foot trod on the human leg in the deep shadows. Not that corpses bothered him unduly, they were all part of a day's or night's work when he had been in the RNLI. It was just the surprise of finding one here. The ravenous crabs must have overlooked it. Maybe it was a drowning, a swimmer who had got into trouble and the tide had washed the body ashore. It was a female, his outstretched probing fingers located small, firm breasts. He grasped an ankle and dragged the corpse unceremoniously into a shaft of moonlight.

The dead girl was beautiful, there was no denying that. Long blonde hair straggled down over her pallid features so that she peeped through the strands at him with wide, dead eyes. She possessed a figure that was as near to perfection as God ever made one. Dugan thought that she was about twenty, maybe even younger.

At first light the crows and gulls would come to breakfast on her. Squabbling over the eyes, pecking and ripping at the unblemished flesh ... unless the crabs found her first.

A moment of sadness, pity that was alien to his nature overwhelmed him and his eyes narrowed thoughtfully. It seemed a sacrilege with one so beautiful, yet she was dead, she wasn't any use to anybody. And if she served a purpose then she wasn't altogether wasted. He pursed his bearded lips. Providence had thrown him a means to kill one of the crustaceans, it would be foolish to spurn manna from the deep.

"Come on, my beauty", he rested his gun up against a rock and bent to lift her. "I reckon you can do a very useful job, and afterwards maybe I'll take you someplace where the soldiers might find you before the gulls get to you."

She was light. He carried her easily across the slippery rocks until he came upon a place – a large rock pool, the moonlight scintillating on its surface – with a shelf set alongside it that might have been made for his very purpose.

Almost reverently he set his burden down upon it, letting her shapely legs dangle in the water, her back resting against a smooth boulder behind her. Her head lolled forwards, there was no way he could prop it up, but it didn't matter. The Sleeping Beauty, he laughed to himself at the thought, waiting for her prince to come. Except that this time the prince would be a regal crab and there was no chance of a crustacean kiss to awaken her.

Dugan went back and fetched his gun; he checked that the lower barrel was loaded with the heavy cartridge. Perfect. He stood surveying the scene he had created; a young girl enjoying a naked midnight bathe. Blissfully unaware that the seabed was crawling with hideous evil monsters. He envisaged them attempting to creep up on her, shambling over the rocks, then hurrying when they smelled her sweet flesh. Jesus Almighty, this young girl was the perfect decoy!

Dugan was skilled in the art of decoying his quarry. In the shed behind the tumbledown cottage where he lived alone were sacks of dummy ducks and woodpigeons. So lifelike that from a distance of a few yards you could not tell them from the living birds; certainly the mallard and woodies couldn't. They came to the lure because there just had to be food where their buddies were feeding, the greedy bastards! Often the unfortunate victims didn't even hear the report of Dugan's shotgun, unaware that they had been fooled. And that was how it was going to be with the crabs. Or, hopefully, just one crab; one that had strayed from the others, come ashore in the hope of finding something that the others had overlooked. And it would find just that, an unwary human, the tender succulent flesh waiting to be shredded and masticated, blood oozing from it like a rare steak.

Dugan settled down facing the dead girl, his back resting against a rock, the gun across his knees. It was a great vantage point up here, he had a field of vision all around, no crab would be able to creep up on him. The sea would reach these rocks, maybe to a depth of a foot or so, a neap tide. Nothing to worry him. In all probability the crabs would come in with it.

His only worry was that there might be a bunch of them, in which case he would have to make a run for the cliff path and hope to beat them to it. No, the main army wouldn't head this way, the cliffs were too steep for them and anyway, they would be concentrating their attack on the town which was well to his left. Just a straggler, perhaps a youngster that had lost its way.

He found himself staring fixedly at the girl, wishing she was alive because then things would have been different and he wouldn't have given a shit about shooting a crab. So lovely, so erotic in her motionless posture. Was it his imagination or had her legs eased apart slightly? A patch of shadow fell across her lower body, and thwarted his voyeuristic pleasure.

She was doing things to him, creating the most pleasurable sensations. With a deliberate effort, he fought them off. He could not afford to relax his vigilance, he was the hunter, he had no wish to become the hunted.

Listening. Those faraway voices were silent now, just the glare of the seafront lights illuminated the sky over Barmouth and the searchlights arced to and fro. The sea was lapping at the rocks, a gentle soothing sound. Dugan glanced at his wristwatch, 2.45am. The tide would begin to ebb in the next half hour. His hopes began to fade, he recalled those moonlight nights when he had crouched in the weeds fringing the pond up in the mountains, straining his ears to catch that first whistle of ducks' wings. Straining and waiting for hours on end until finally he had to accept that the mallard were not going to fly tonight. Anticipation blending into disappointment, psyched up and then let down.

By 3.30am he knew it was going to be like that now. The tide was ebbing and the crabs had not shown up. He was suddenly aware of his tiredness, almost exhausted once he accepted that his vigil had been fruitless. His dead companion was hidden by the shadows, just a pale blur that might have been anything, not even erotic anymore.

Slowly he stood up and without glancing back, climbed down onto the wet sand. His decoy had been perfect but she had not lured his quarry – which was often the way of the hunt. Tomorrow it might be different but he would not have the girl then.

He thought about taking her back with him, then changed his mind. She was dead. Whatever might happen to her body would not make any difference to her. Dragging his feet, he set off in the direction of the hidden cliff path, the gun seemingly a ten kilo weight resting on his shoulder.

And then he saw the crab. It was crouching about ten yards from the cliff face, motionless and watching him. At least, it had to be watching him even though its tiny, hideous face was bathed in shadow because it was facing him. For a moment his heart skipped a beat and any icy tingle ran up the base of his neck and spread into his scalp. Then relief – and he almost laughed out loud. It was just a baby, the one he had been willing to appear throughout his long wait on the rocks.

It was no bigger than a terrier. There were maybe bigger normal crabs than this one in the oceans of the world. Dugan swung the gun off his shoulder, pushed the rifle lever across, flipped up the peep sight and took a bead on his intended victim. Just a dark mass, almost hidden against the cliff. He lowered the gun, advanced another two or three steps. This bastard was nothing to be afraid of, his only concern was that the heavy bullet might shatter it and render it useless for either meat or a trophy. But that was a chance he would have to take.

"Hold it right there, pal!" He was still unable to focus on its features in the sight, to judge where they were. A range of fifteen yards, no more. He took a trigger pressure.

The report was deafening, the recoil threw him back a couple of feet. His fear was that he might have missed but even as the twin barrels were jerked skywards by the force of the shot, he saw the crab disintegrate, blown apart. The shell shattered, fragments flew in all directions and clinked on the pebble beach like falling shrapnel. The decimated remnants of the crustacean body rolled over and lay still.

Dugan's first reaction was one of relief combined with euphoria. *I got the bastard!* Then realisation came with the wafts of powder smoke from the gun in his hands; the futility of it all. A shot-blasted crab corpse that was no use to anybody, the meat strung along the shore for scavenging birds to feast on, the fragmented shell …

He stared, his shoulders bowed and starting to throb from the recoil! *Oh Jesus, I fucked it up!*

Dimly aware of sounds – the lapping of the tide, seabirds protesting at the nocturnal disturbance – that searchlight trying to pick him out, but the jutting headland keeping it at bay. And something else …

Click-click, clickety-click.

Even then he was not fully aware of the advancing crab until it was too late. He tried to flee but his feet refused to move. The gun fell from his grasp and clanked loudly on a stone. He watched the oncoming crustacean with numb disbelief, noting how it towered over him as its pincers reached out for him. A monstrous creature materialising out of the shadows.

And in those last few seconds of life Dugan knew and cursed his humiliation. Yelling his frustration as he was lifted aloft, he hated this crab for the ease with which it had lured him to his death … decoyed him with its own dead offspring.

The crab began to feed.

REVENGE

A quest for revenge leads to terrible consequences

Klin was sweating profusely as he pulled the boat up on the rocky beach of the small island. He shaded his eyes against the glare of the afternoon sun and stared back out to sea. Even a fisherman of his experience and calibre could not hold back the tiny shivers which ran up his spine and neck as he saw the cruel coral reefs, half-submerged beneath the water. Five hundred yards of them, a maze that protected this tiny island from casual visitors, claimed the lives of the unwary. There were few men who would have made it, would have had the courage to risk it. And Klin was one of those.

Tall and rangy, he topped six feet, his bronze muscular body clad only in a tattered pair of khaki shorts, a pair of scuffed sandals his only other attire. An unkempt mane of jet black beard tumbled down his broad chest, hiding features that were handsome in a wild sort of way. It was impossible to judge his age to within fifteen years, but if you looked closely you saw flecks of grey in the dark hair, a wrinkle in the mahogany skin. But it was his eyes you noticed most of all, dark like the rest of him, penetrating, reading more of you than you read of him. And you felt uncomfortable in his presence for no reason that you could logically define. You dropped your gaze and admitted to yourself that in some inexplicable way you were afraid of this man. You didn't like him, but you respected him.

Klin turned back, surveyed the island, the almost impenetrable mangrove swamp that had grown back since the last time he had set foot on this uncharted scrap of wasteland ten years ago. He recalled the fire that had ravaged it, started by his own hand, the wall of flames that swept terrifyingly inland, finally destroying those …

He grimaced at the memory of the giant crustaceans, the huge killer crabs which had ravaged the Great Barrier Reef, armoured invincible monsters that had virtually destroyed the millionaire paradise of Hayman Island in their insatiable hatred of mankind and their relentless craving for human flesh and blood. A long time ago but Klin would never forget; sometimes they came back to him in his nightmares, like castanets the clicking of their pincers, sheer malevolence burning out of their tiny eyes. Many was the time that he had awoken screaming, his flesh dripping with sweat, staring into the darkness of his beach hut and telling himself that it was only another dream. They weren't there, they couldn't be because the fire had destroyed them all. And even when he had harnessed logic and dispersed the terrible fantasies of the nocturnal hours he still had his doubts. And during the last few weeks those doubts had crept back and now he knew that the killer crabs were alive again, that some of them had survived and bred. And once again, they were hungry for human flesh and blood; they remembered and wanted a terrible revenge for what Man had done to them. That was why Klin had come back to this island.

They had got that girl off the beach on Hayman Island on the last full moon, a young millionairess who got her kicks out of nude bathing. She had gone down to the water just after midnight; Klin had observed from the doorway of his hut and it had done exciting things to him, reminded him of another beautiful rich girl who had once figured in his life. Caroline du Brunner had been a crab victim and now this other girl was asking for trouble. No, not from the crabs because they were all dead years ago but from inshore killer sharks and there were plenty of them about this summer.

Klin watched her swim right out, almost yielded to temptation and went down to the water to join her. She would have liked that, pretended at first that she wasn't going to let a common fisherman … But she'd change her mind, women always did where Klin was concerned. Maybe if he had gone then she wouldn't be dead now. Or else, they would both be dead. He grinned wryly to himself.

She had swum back to the beach, come up out of the tide, lithe and sensuous, shaking herself like a dog. And the next second they had got her. There were just two of them, as big as cows, moving with deceptive speed. Maybe if she had run she might have escaped their lumbering charge but instead she froze to the spot. The crustaceans got her by the legs first, snapped one and amputated the other, the blood from the ragged stump spouting thick and dark in the wan moonlight. She fell forward and they stood back and let her thrash and crawl a yard or so; Klin sensed their unholy gloating, their delight at her agony. Then they were on her again, pincers moving in obscenely and opening her thighs wide, making her do the splits, wrenching her limbs out of their sockets. A tender shapely breast was snapped off neatly, the soft flesh conveyed to a waiting mouth. In the stillness between the screams Klin heard the slurping, the munching, heaved at the revolting gluttony of creatures that had no right to live on this planet.

Those claws were gigantic scalpels in the hands of a butcherous surgeon carrying out an abdominal operation, slitting her open from crotch to throat, blood spraying the crabs as they delved into the incision and pulled out yards of intestine, sucking it up like tripe out of a barrel. Their appetite was whetted, the foregames were over.

Her screams grew fainter until finally they ceased. Now she was just a dismembered heap of bloody flesh. Unrecognisable for what she had once been, the power of her riches futile against these behemoths from out of the ocean. The crabs fed, crunched the bones and masticated noisily. Klin looked back towards the Royal Hayman Hotel; lights shone from every window and faint strains of an orchestra tuning up reached his ears from an open ballroom window. Nobody had heard the girl's screams, and if they had they couldn't have given a shit, Klin reflected, because it wasn't them that were getting mangled up, even if there were killer crabs in the sea then what the hell. Maybe most of them had never even read what happened here once and in any case, they would be gone by the end of the week. The crabs were somebody else's problem.

Klin reflected why he had not done anything. Not that the girl could have been saved once the crabs got her. Maybe he should have raised the alarm. But he didn't and only now, standing here on the beach of the most dangerous island in Australia's Great Barrier Reef, did he understand why he hadn't. Because he had a personal score to settle with the monsters; he hated them as much as they hated mankind! Maybe there were only a few of the bastards, the beginnings of a new strain of mutants, and if that was the case then that was swell. Whatever, he had to get them himself, the way that he, Professor Davenport and Shannon of the Shark Patrol, the biggest bullshitter on Hayman, had once done. This time it had to be Klin's own show. He had a score to settle; they had snatched Caroline du Brunner from him, left him the way he had always been, a womaniser without a woman. And, Jesus Christ, they'd pay for that!

I'm getting crazier in my old age, he told himself as he beached the boat, lifted out the double-barrel .500 Express that had once belonged to Harvey Logan, a big-game hunter who had called in at Hayman and thought he was going to bag himself a crab trophy. The rifle had proved inadequate, a toy would have served as well, but somehow it gave Klin a feeling of reassurance. It bucked and you heard the slug whine, heard it strike and ricochet. You didn't feel so vulnerable. I'm crazy, he decided as he walked up the sloping beach and remembered that suitcase full of money that was still buried amongst the pines behind the hotel. It had been Frank Burke's ill-gotten loot, which in turn had been stolen by the girl who called herself Caroline du Brunner. She was a con girl, but it didn't matter because by the time she got her hands on that money she was already as wealthy as the image she had created. Thanks to the crabs that dough had come Klin's way. After it was all over he could have sailed right out of Barbecue Bay to a life of ease. Wealth would only have taken the challenge out of life, he had told himself, but that was not the real reason he had stayed on. These crabs had become an obsession, he would never get them out of his system until he had killed the last one with his own hands. Moonlit nights he got thinking about them most, a kind of masochistic worship that kept him on Barbecue Bay, just waiting.

Until Now.

This island hadn't changed any, Klin noted. He remembered seeing it from the Patrol's chopper that time, roughly circular, its shores bounded by treacherous coral reefs. The swamp was spread over most of it, patches of water visible here and there, most of the land hidden by an impenetrable tangle of mangroves. A mangrove swamp can grow up in a few years, the seedlings sometimes drifting for hundreds of miles with the current, capable of remaining alive for a year, even longer, sprouting additional roots and top growth whilst afloat. Then they get washed up somewhere, take root and spread. Like they had done on this island that didn't even have a name and where nobody came because of the reefs. Beneath the top foliage was dead dry wood that would blaze and start a forest fire once you got it going. That was what happened here before. It had been Davenport's idea once they had found out that the crabs were spawning here. Let 'em all come up out of the ocean, big ones carrying their young on their backs the way crustaceans do; let 'em get right into the heart of the swamp and then set the whole island on fire from different points. A gigantic ring of flames that even the crabs could not get through. Jesus, Klin still heard their rage and pain as the fire got them, roasting them alive. But they hadn't got the Big One, the one they called Queen Crab. She had been blinded but she had not died. Maybe there had been a male lurking somewhere in the ocean depths and they had got together, made out and started the whole thing off once more. Klin lit a cheroot, rattled his box of matches; the sound was reassuring, as reassuring as the weight of Harvey Logan's gun under his arm because the big fisherman knew exactly what he had to do. An old motto of his "What you've done once, you can do again." And by Christ, if he didn't do just that he was going to finish up as crab-bait for sure.

The mangroves had drifted in again after the fire and repopulated the island just like the crabs had done. The scenery was as familiar as if it was only yesterday when Shannon had put the chopper down and Davenport had said, "this is the place all right." And now it was the place again.

The narrow waterway was still there, the water no deeper than a few inches, the bed thick mud and coral, the mangrove branches overhead shutting out the sunlight and creating its own atmosphere of gloomy eeriness, restricting visibility to a few yards. In places the water was a dark red colour caused by the tannic acid from the mangroves.

Klin's progress was slow, stopping to listen at frequent intervals but there was no sound other than the distant muffled waves on the coral. He did not expect to hear anything else for it was only mid-afternoon and the crabs would not move until the moon rose. But he needed time; time to build his fires, a task that several men had completed last time and one that he must now carry out single-handed. Not so thorough, more chancy, because he must rely on the flames spreading from one starting point for he would not have time to circle the island lighting individual crustacean funeral pyres. He must rely on the wind and there was precious little of that.

Klin built his first fire a quarter of a mile into the mangrove forest. The crabs would doubtless follow this watercourse and he would have to try to cut off their retreat whilst the flames got a hold. He had just finished when his ears picked up a faint noise, one that had his heartbeat speeding up, every whipcord muscle in his body tensing. A clicking, a long way away … Relief as he recognised the sound, just the clicking of small, ordinary crabs scuttling away through the undergrowth at his approach. God, he was edgy.

The foul stench of decay was stifling, the heat intense and overpowering, his body awash with sweat. It had him thinking about that hidden money again … there was still time to cut and run, to leave this place and forget that it had ever existed. But he knew he would stay, that forces beyond his ken had called him here just as they had called the crabs. He was a puppet in the hand of Fate.

At length he reached the big clearing. It was maybe a hundred yards in circumference, a sheet of stagnant reddish-brown water where for some reason the mangroves had not rooted, a foul stinking lake. And it was to this place that he knew the crabs would come clicking their way in the silvery moonlight, the place where he must trap them and burn them. His pulses pounded at the thought and his dark eyes took on an expression that was maniacal as his obsession neared its peak.

He savoured his own hate, the malignant driving force that burned up logic and clear thinking. He stood there for maybe half an hour, a clairvoyant viewing future happenings and lusting in what he saw. He smelled the smoke, felt the intense heat from the crackling flames as they leapt from one tree to another, a circle of fire consuming everything in its path. He heard the shrill cries of the trapped crabs, their squeals of pain and fear, heard their flesh sizzling. There was a pain in his chest but he ignored it; his vision was blurred because of the smoke which smarted his eyes and his dizziness was due to the suffocating atmosphere.

Then his fantasy was gone and he knew there was work to be done, piles of dead wood to be assembled, and when the time came he must sprint like the torch-bearer from Olympia had once done, pushing his brand into each tinder-dry heap; then back down the watercourse, lighting the final fire, running and hoping that he would make it back to his boat in time. Pausing on the beach to fire round after round back into the swamp from Harvey Logan's .500 Express, a final defiant gesture of victory. Shouting, "it was Klin that did this, you bastards, d'you hear me, it was Klin!"

Then he was busy, oblivious of the heat and the stench, gathering dead branches and piling them up, relishing his task and only finishing it when darkness dropped its curtain over the island … then he took up his position some fifty yards from where that sluggish stream oozed its way out of the forest, and waited. In one sweaty hand he held the gun, in the other his matches.

Just waiting and listening. And hoping that his intuition had not let him down and that the crabs would come as they had come ten years ago, a shambling army that would be defeated in a fiery hell.

The moon was almost at its zenith when Klin heard them coming, the muffled clicking growing louder by the second, a scraping of many pincers on coral. He tensed, peered into the shadows, mentally urging the monsters to come this way.

Then he saw them, silhouettes in the ethereal light, creatures that seemed far bigger than when he had last seen them, ungainly as they bore their offspring aloft, all making for …

Oh, merciful God, they weren't heading into that foul swamp lake, they were fanning out into the forest itself, finding a dozen tiny tributaries, going into those godawful everglades! Realisation numbed Klin, had him cursing incoherently, trying to will his enemy back into the clearing, but nothing would deter the crabs from their destination.

Click-click-clickety-click.

He could have pressed himself back against the bole of any one of a dozen mangrove trees around him, climbed up into their boughs and been safe, but Klin dispelled any thought of skulking the night hours away. His fury was already beginning to erupt into a terrible rage, the hunter thwarted when his plans had seemed foolproof, crustacean cunning outwitting the guile of Man. For they knew, Jesus Christ, they knew, had sensed this trap through an instinct evolved from their ancestors who had perished here; they saw the dangers of the lake, headed away from it where they could not be trapped by fire.

And above all, they smelled an enemy in their midst, scented Man in their domain!

The Big One was there leading them, Klin recognised the Queen Crab by her very size, a giant amongst giants, a leader upon which the rest fawned. Pincers aloft, antennae waving, searching the shadows for Klin just as he had been scanning them for her. A pincer circled, pointed into the dense mangroves and he knew that his hiding place had been discovered!

Perhaps he could have run, stumbled away from them in the darkness, made it back to the boat. The thought did not enter his enraged brain for never would he flee in the face of a foe. The matchbox fell from his fingers, rattled once in its futility as it struck the ground. And then the rifle came up to his shoulder, Klin's blurred vision seeking and finding a sight in the uncertain light. The big female, her gargoyle-like face lit up by the red glow from her eyes, triumph and hatred merging in her contorted expression. There he is, the one who burned us before. Take him and feast on his flesh and blood.

The report of the .500 was blanketed by the thick mangrove forest, a dull clap of thunder rolling through the trees trying to find a way out, the flash sheet lightning that lit up the entire scene, magnified it a hundredfold. Impact – the heavy slug finding its mark on the flesh beneath the shell, a dull thud, the crab seeming to check but only momentarily. A crustacean scream of rage and hate, crabs coming from all sides, answering the cry of the one who controlled their every movement.

Klin fired again, reloaded, discharged both barrels, the recoil throwing him back against a twisted tree trunk. The smell of burned cordite was sharp in his lungs, the pain in his shoulder seeming to spread across into his chest, a rippling agony that robbed him of the strength to lift his weapon but somehow he still managed to reload. This time he fired from the hip, the gun bucking, the hammers gouging his hand viciously so that blood rushed from a severed vein.

The iron stench of human blood, how those crabs scented it, came at him in a shambling invincible wave. Still firing, the force of the bullets chipping their protective shells but not stopping them.

And then the final impact took Klin in the chest, a bone-shattering blow that threw him back into the mud so that he lay there looking up at the mangrove canopy above him, tracing patterns with his failing eyesight where the moonbeams made a criss-cross over his head; breathless, writhing, wondering what in hell they had fired back at him. A missile of some kind, somehow they had learned how to propel it accurately and with such force that it was capable of shattering a human breastbone. Oh God, the pain was excruciating …

The moonlight was fading, blackness tinged with red creeping in, numbing him so that he scarcely felt it when his outstretched legs were seized. Just mental agony, seeing again that girl being ripped apart on the beach back on Hayman Island, mutilated beyond recognition, then every last shred of her eaten so that the searchers found nothing and blamed it on the sharks.

Cursing. Then laughing hysterically at the irony of it all when everything began to fade and he felt himself starting to fall into the yawning bottomless chasm beneath him. Klin, the hunter of Barbecue Bay, had fallen into his own trap but nobody would ever know. The islanders wouldn't be able to bloody well laugh at him because … oh shit, you should have told the Shark Patrol and had this place blasted to hell. No, it is hell and I wouldn't have had it any other way.

He mustered up one last laugh and hoped they heard and understood, knew that he had not gone down screaming at the last.

THE VIGIL

Nowhere is safe when the crabs are on the rampage

"They can't get us in here … can they?" the youth asked.

"I dunno," Billington replied, letting his gaze rove around the interior of the blockhouse, wrinkled his nose at the stench of urine and excreta, the soil floor a carpet of litter, empty ring cans and broken bottles. He noticed a used French letter lying almost apologetically across a crisp packet like a slug that had crawled on it in search of scraps and been killed by the salt. Christ, you had to be pretty desperate to fuck in a place like this; you had to be desperate to come in here at all. They were, all four of them. He switched his gaze to the girl with the young child. She was damnably attractive in spite of the pallor of her features and her dirt-stained bikini. He could have fucked her in here all right, given the chance. Who knows, he might get that chance. There was no way of knowing how long they were going to be cooped up in here.

"It's awful," the girl felt that she had to say something. "This place stinks, it's no place to bring a child. You could catch some awful disease amongst all this filth."

"You could catch a lot worse out there," Billington tried to make a joke out of it but it did not sound funny. Nothing was funny anymore. "We're lucky. There's an awful lot of folks less lucky than us out there." Because they're dead, ripped to pieces and eaten by crabs as big as cows that nobody believed existed until they came up out of the sea.

Silence. Billington's thoughts went back a few hours, to just around midday. A crowded holiday beach on the Welsh coast, a heatwave that the experts forecast was going to break by tomorrow. Crowds, kids laughing and yelling, building castles and paddling, doing all the things that children did on a holiday beach. He had been stretched out on the soft sand, eyeing up that bird a few yards away, considering chatting her up. She had a kid but there was no sign of a husband. Perhaps her marriage had broken up. He was trying to figure out a way of approaching her when all hell had broken loose.

People were screaming, fleeing out of the tide in blind panic. And the giant crabs were coming in their hundreds, behemoths that moved fast in their lust for human flesh and blood. A half-moon attack, planned with uncanny military precision so that scores of holidaymakers had their retreat cut off, herded into a circle and slaughtered by those vicious pincers. Their bodies ripped apart, the monsters fighting amongst themselves over severed limbs, masticating with a revolting squelching noise.

Some made it to the headland. If Billington had chosen to sunbathe nearer to the Marine Parade he would probably have made it too. But the crustaceans had blocked that escape route from further down the wide golden sands. Behind were sheer unscaleable cliffs and way beyond the coastline levelled out again. A mile at the most, if you ran like hell you might just make it. On his own he might have done but he had stopped to help that auburn-haired girl and her child and that slowed them up, giving the crabs time to deploy another unit. Trapped!

Then he had spied the blockhouse, an old wartime fortification at the end of the cliffs, a concrete pillbox whose only use these last thirty years had been as a beach toilet. Slitted windows and a narrow entrance. Their only chance, the bastards wouldn't be able to reach them in there. At least he didn't think so.

It was only when they reached the blockhouse that Billington was aware that the youth had tagged on to them, an eighteen year-old wearing only a pair of frayed and filthy jeans. Resentment, because even in the midst of this carnage Billington was thinking about the girl. He had saved her, so far at least, and she would have to be grateful for it. Play your cards carefully, we're going to be stuck in this stink-hole for some time.

He wished he had a watch. It was difficult to determine the passing of time but looking out through the nearest vent he judged it had to be early evening. The tide was in, damn it, and there were still crabs about. "How much longer are we going to have to stay here?" The youth was scared to hell, biting his fingernails. "Surely they'll come and get us out before long. There are coastguard choppers flying up and down all the while."

"They won't come for us because they don't know we're here," Billington thought he sounded supercilious. "And without going outside we've no way of letting them know. If you want to try it, son, that's up to you, but there's a crab in the edge of the tide about twenty yards away and he knows we're in here. Me, I'm going to sit it out with the lady here but you please yourself. You don't have to take orders from me."

"I'm thirsty and hungry."

Now that was a damn-fool thing to say, sitting here in the stifling heat and stench with empty coke and beer cans and a litter of crisp bags mocking you like an oasis mirage in the middle of the desert. A reminder that they could have done without. The girl winced, closed her eyes, and the child began to cry again.

"What's your name?" Billington tried to change the subject.

"Frank." A sullen reply.

"Mine's Marie," she made a valiant attempt to smile, "and this is Emma, Mr ...?"

"Billington," he forgot the crabs for a moment. "Ed."

"Do ... do you think we'll make it.?"

"Well, they can't get at us in here and they can't just sit out there forever waiting for us to come out. It isn't as though we're in some remote place. There's a town less than a mile and a half away teeming with troops. We'll have to sit it out for a few hours but once the tide's gone out the crabs'll have to go with it because they can't live on dry land." At least I hope they can't. "It's just a question of being patient. We were bloody fools to come to the beach after what happened at Shell Island last night. The authorities should have closed all the beaches."

"I don't think even they really believed it," she replied. "Crabs as big as cows. But it's real enough, we've seen it for ourselves."

"Maybe your husband will come looking for you?" A loaded question, the thing he wanted to know most of all.

"I don't have a husband. He left me two years ago, when Emma was barely twelve months old. We're trying for a reconciliation but it won't work, I know it won't."

Ed Billington's pulses raced. Maybe in a backhanded way these crabs had done him a big favour. "You stick close to me, we'll get out of this. Frank here can please himself. He can either stay or try and make a run for it. He's old enough to make up his own mind what he's going to do."

Frank stared balefully but did not answer. Flies buzzed, found some excreta and settled on it to feed. It seemed hotter than ever now and you found yourself drawing breath consciously, your body lathered with sweat. Golden evening sunlight slanted on the filthy floor, scintillated on a crumpled Pepsi can. You're thirsty, aren't you? You'll be even thirstier before this lot is over.

"This is stupid." Frank stood up, went to the nearest window. "I can't see any crabs. They've all gone. A couple of hundred yards and you're on grass, a field. They can't follow you then."

"You please yourself, son. As I said, you're big enough to make up your own mind. Don't let me stop you if you want to go." Fuck off and leave us to it. Billington's eyes alighted on another crumpled French letter amidst the garbage and he knew he was going to get an erection. He knew also that the youth was going to try and make a break for it.

It was about another ten minutes before Frank stated in a voice that quavered, "I'm going to leave you to it."

Frank hesitated, swallowed, and then he went, a rush that took him out through the narrow doorway.

"Oh God!" Marie muttered and held Emma close to her.

Billington crossed to the nearest window from where he had a narrow view of the beach outside, a line of sand and shingle with the evening tide lapping at it. So natural, so peaceful. He was aware of Marie at his shoulder, felt her tenseness, the way she caught her breath, afraid to look but compelled to.

Frank was sprinting, heedless of the sharp shingle, slowing when he came to a patch of soft sand. The tide came right in here in a kind of miniature estuary. He would have to wade for maybe three or four yards, and then he would be safe.

"He's going to make it," she breathed. "Ed, maybe if we went, too, and ..." Her voice trailed off, gave way to a shrill scream of terror.

The crab had been lurking in that patch of water, totally submerged, as though it knew it was the track the humans would take if they made a break for it. It surfaced, a hideous living U-boat, antennae waving menacingly, claws spread wide, sweeping inwards. Frank screamed just once before he was guillotined, an instant decapitation that plopped the bloody head into the water, the trunk spouting crimson blood as it was lifted aloft and borne towards those cavernous jaws.

The horrified watchers saw the headless body being stuffed into the mouth, the slurping of flesh that still quivered, the grinding and snapping of frail bones. The creature crouched there munching, tiny red eyes that seemed to penetrate the interior of the blockhouse. Seeing and understanding. You can't escape, we'll get you in the end.

Billington thought Marie was going to faint, slipped an arm around her. Emma was awake and crying. And inside the concrete building it seemed more stifling than ever, those empty drink cans grinning at them in the sunshine. You're trapped. You'll die of thirst if the crabs don't get you. Nobody will come to help you.

"It was horrible," Marie sank down to her knees cradled Emma in her lap. "I … don't believe it. It's some kind of nightmare and any minute we'll wake up."

They stayed like that, squatting amidst the filth of what had become a beach lavatory over the years, just looking at each other until the dusk crept in and reduced them to silhouettes. Neither of them spoke because there was nothing to say; their predicament was clear enough. Listening, hearing the gentle swish of the sea on the beach, gulls calling, and somewhere there was sporadic gunfire.

Billington's thoughts returned to Marie. Just himself, her and the kid. Fate had thrown together his earlier fantasies in a macabre way. They were going to spend a night together but not in the way he had dreamed.

"I'm sorry about your marriage," he was glad really but it was a starting point. Go on, tell me the lurid details.

"We weren't suited," she answered him out of the darkness and there was a note of sadness in her voice. "We both realised that, but we were trying to make it work out for the sake of Emma. This holiday was to be a break apart whilst we thought things over. We're getting together again next week, but it's a waste of time really. We had to give it a go though. How about you?"

"My wife was killed two years ago." Damn it, she was drawing him out, making him talk about something he wanted to forget. Best get it over and done with, though. "A runaway lorry ploughed into a queue of people waiting for a bus. Two killed … she was one of them."

"I'm sorry."

So am I. Nobody will replace her, not even you. But a man has to have a woman and I've been too long without. "I got made redundant a fortnight later. I thought I might as well kill time here as lounge about at home. I've put the house up for sale. I don't know what I'm going to do."

"Do … do you think there's any chance for us, Ed?"

"There's a chance." He said. "Provided we don't do anything stupid like young Frank. Hell, we're safe enough in here, we've just got to sit it out. Tomorrow, the next day, who knows?"

"The heat, the lack of food and water's going to knock Emma about," she groaned.

There was no answer to that.

"What are you going to do when we get out of here?" She just stopped herself from saying "if".

"No plans," he smiled to himself in the blackness. "I guess I'd like to give you a call if things don't work out for you."

"They won't," she replied, and then he felt her hand slipping into his. Crazy, he thought, I could have spent hours trying to chat her up on the beach and got nowhere but this has thrown us together.

"I'll think of something tomorrow," he yawned. "Maybe when the tide's far enough out so that no crabs are lurking close by I'll climb up on the roof and holler like hell. Somebody's bound to hear us and then they'll send a chopper to lift us out."

"You really think you can?" New hope, squeezing his hand tightly.

"I reckon," he answered, and let his head rest on her shoulder. "At least we can sleep secure in the knowledge that the crabs can't get in here. Christ, one would have a job to fit inside here if the roof was off."

Gradually they slid into an uneasy sleep.

* * *

Strange dreams haunted Marie. Ed was with her in a strange place, a crowded street where a guillotine loomed over them with evil purposefulness, blood dripping steadily from its mighty blade. And all around them were wizened old hags clad in filthy tattered attire, blood red headscarves tied down tightly over their heads. They were knitting with a sinister urgency whilst the blood continued to drip from that instrument of barbaric execution.

Click-click-clickety-click-click.

Drip…drip…splat…drip.

Click-clickety-click-click.

A sea of ghoulish faces were turned towards herself and this man who had been a total stranger only hours ago. Toothless cavities mouthed mute obscenities. *You're going to die, just like your child has. That's her blood dripping now!*

Sheer panic had her fighting to surface from the depths of that nightmare, clawing her way out of the darkness into a stifling, stinking, filthy octagonal hovel where bright moonlight sparkled on a pile of empty cans. Ed was here, fast asleep against her; she groped for Emma but the child was not there. *No, it was only a dream, she has to be here.* She wasn't.

Click-click-clickety-click.

The sound filled the blockhouse like the aimless clicking of castanets, a thousand knitting needles working tirelessly. And in the shadows something moved, lurched. Marie drew back, saw those tiny glowing red pinpoints, felt their malevolence boring into her. She made out a face, a horrible wizened hag-like countenance with the mouth moving, pouting, munching. Swallowing. Slurping.

Tin cans rolled, rattled metallically. A shell-shape, about the size of a large Alsatian dog, legs that scraped and gouged the concrete floor as it moved. Another behind it. And another. She knew in that instant that this was no crazy figment of a terrified brain, that it was stark reality. The crabs had found a way in and they had taken Emma, eaten her right down to the last shred of her tender flesh!

Ed Billington was stirring, seeming to have difficulty in dragging himself out of his exhausted slumber. She wanted to shake him, to scream in his ear, "You were wrong, Ed. They got in, they've eaten Emma," but no words would come. Paralytic with terror she could only watch, in her own mind she had already surrendered, was offering herself as a blood sacrifice to these crustacean killers from the deep.

"Jesus God Almighty!" Billington threw off the last dregs of sleep, sat bolt upright. His brain spun, he wanted to apologise to the girl by his side. *I was wrong, we should have risked it, made a run for it. At least that way we'd have gone down in the open. We're trapped. Here we don't stand a chance, not as much as that poor bugger Frank.*

"They got Emma," Marie was surprised how calmly she spoke when her vocal chords functioned again. "At least it was quick. She never even screamed."

He nodded, asked himself one question and came up with the answer. *How? How did they get inside?*

"They're small buggers," he grunted. "Little giant crabs. Why didn't I think of it before? They can't all be big, they have to be small sometime before they start to grow!"

Four crabs, bloody infantile entrails spilling from their mouths, squatted there looking at the two humans against the wall. Tiny eyes blazed hate and arrogance.

There was no way their prey could escape them in here.

THE SURVIVOR

Will the monstrous crustaceans that have terrorised the oceans of the world for decades ever be exterminated?

"Hamish has started punting again," there was a note of resentment in Donald Brown's voice as he surveyed the Solway estuary through his binoculars from the window of his cottage. "Everything's back to normal now, I guess. The ghouls and sight seers have tired of searching the banks at low tide for souvenirs. I guess every splinter of crab shell and that World War II bomb have been found. The geese and duck have returned and that old bugger, Hamish, is back so it's time I was out there, too."

"He's harmless enough," Rosie, clad in denim jacket and jeans which were way overdue for the washing machine, clutched at her husband's arm. "You be careful going out there, Donald. You can't guarantee that explosion destroyed all of those crabs."[1]

"If it hadn't then they'd surely have had some of those souvenir hunters by now. I'll get the punt ready and make a start at daylight tomorrow, get out there before that silly old fucker disturbs every duck and goose between Glenkirk and Glencaple."

He moved through to the small living room where the television was running. Rosie had it on most of the day, not that she really watched it. It was a kind of company during the long hours she spent alone. If Donald wasn't out shooting then he was up in the spare bedroom which was

---

[1] See Killer Crabs: The Return

where he did all his own hobby chores. Like a kid playing in the nursery.

* * *

It was a misty November morning as Donald pushed the gunning punt out into the current, clambering aboard and lying flat behind the big gun. He loaded it, a charge of black powder, wadding and quarter of a pound of shot. The old 12-bore was by his side, his 'cripple stopper' to deal with any birds which had not been killed outright.

The tide was ebbing, visibility was poor. Any wildfowl were unlikely to spot the grey painted punt until it was too late.

He let the craft drift, did not bother sculling. Somewhere up ahead he could hear the 'pink-pink' of geese which had roosted on a sandbank and were just awakening. With the coming of daylight they would flight out to the fields to feed. He needed to catch them before they left.

Then he saw them, a flock of about twenty, stretching their wings and honking to welcome a new day. Two hundred yards, maybe a little more. He needed to drift closer, 75–80 would be fine for the big gun.

He raised his head slowly, ducked down again. A hundred yards now. His fingers closed over the lanyard which fired the gun. Don't rush it.

One goose took off, honking its way downstream. The rest were making ready to follow. It was now or never.

The six-foot barrel belched flame, its mighty recoil pushing the lightweight craft backwards. A cloud of sulphur smelling, black smoke hung over the water, obscuring Donald's vision. Wingbeats, honking, alarmed quacking from some duck. When the smoke dispersed Donald saw the result of his shot. Five or six Pinkfeet geese were lying motionless in the mud, another three were on their backs, feebly flapping their last. Two were wounded, swimming in the water fifty yards away.

Donald grabbed the shotgun, cocked the hammers and took aim. Two shots rang out, more black powder smoke wafted in front but when it cleared he saw the geese floating motionless. He sculled forward and retrieved both geese. Six dead on the mudbank along with a couple of mallard and a shelduck. A good morning's work, all he had to do now was to retrieve them. He moved in close to the bank.

And that was when he saw the crab!

He stared at it in disbelief. It was big, some three and a half feet in length with a width of at least two feet. Half buried in the mud, it was not moving. No, it wasn't big, it was a little'un, a baby from those monsters which the World War II bomb had blown to smithereens.

With no small amount of trepidation he leaned across, grabbed hold of a pincer and pulled. God, it took some shifting, finally squelching out of the mud. Part of its shell was chipped, proof that it had felt the force of that explosion. Stunned, it had lived for a while before dying a slow death recently. If it had been dead for weeks it would have stank. Donald sniffed. It smelled fresh enough.

Donald's eye for business took over. MacPherson, the butcher and fishmonger who bought his shot wildfowl, would almost certainly buy this crab. He was a miserly old sod and you had to haggle with him. Take it or leave it, Mac, Jock Kerr in Dumfries will buy it. MacPherson would come to a compromise for sure, he had a long standing feud with his rival.

Slowly but surely Donald loaded up the punt, the crab in the bottom, geese and ducks piled on top of it. It was going to be a risky trip home, he would have to wait for the tide to turn, float with it. He didn't want to lose his cargo. Nor his life.

* * *

"Where the hell've you been?" Rosie opened the front door, stood there arms akimbo, an expression of mingled relief and anger on her broad features. "I thought mebbe you'd gone and drowned. What's that you've got there?"

"A crab," he was struggling to drag it from the beached punt to the dilapidated wooden shed at the rear of the cottage. "A bloody big 'un. Must've bin injured in the blast, somehow survived afore dying in the last day or so."

"And what the hell are you going to do with it?" She eyed the crustacean with suspicion.

"Sell it to MacPherson, or Kerr, if he won't offer a decent price. Failing that I'll clean out the shell and offer it as a souvenir, put it on eBay."

"You're bloody crazy," she turned away and went back indoors.

* * *

Donald was urgently in need of a supply of shotgun cartridges for the 12-bore; he had less than half-a-dozen left. He reloaded his fired cases, an easy enough task even though it meant recharging them singly. A full evening's work but that was fine by him. The alternative was sitting in the living room with Rosie and the telly.

He was a heavy cigarette smoker and Rosie objected strongly. Roll-ups and strong tobacco, he was rarely without a fag in his mouth even when he was reloading cartridges.

He just had to take care that he didn't drop a spark in the open can of black gunpowder.

Tonight, he decided, he would load every empty cartridge case which he had, maybe thirty or so. That would occupy him for most of the evening. It was a pleasant enough chore.

He rolled a cigarette, drew deeply on it and exhaled twin streams of smoke. He checked his tools, powder and shot measures, rammer for seating the wads firmly in the tubes, and then opened a new 5lb can of black powder.

He re-lit his roll-up and began his evening's work. Tomorrow he would make a trip into Dumfries, see what MacPherson would offer him for the crab. He always got geese cheap because the sale of dead wild geese was illegal and he had to use his own discreet outlets. If Don had known who those customers were then he would have sold the birds direct to them.

But Mac was certainly not having the crab for peanuts. No way.

What was that? Donald paused in the act of pouring pellets into a partly-filled cartridge case, listened. There it went again, a noise like timber being smashed up with a heavy instrument. Crash, bang, crash.

It seemed to be coming from the direction of the old shed behind the house. He had taken the precaution of padlocking the door just in case those yobbos from the village were lucking around on a dark evening with sod-all else to do. Thompson's lawnmower had mysteriously disappeared a few weeks ago.

The sound of splintering wood came again only this time much closer. Like it was down at the bottom of the stairs. Then came a scream, a long drawn out one that ended abruptly. It could only have come from Rosie.

What the hell was going on down there?

Donald leapt to his feet, dragged the ill-fitting door wide and then he was staring in horror and disbelief. The scene below him in the hall was like a crazed nightmare. It could not possibly be anything else.

The front door had been reduced to matchwood and beneath the debris lay Rosie. Or what remained of her. Above her, pinning her to the floor was that crab, tearing ferociously at the human flesh which it had bared, shredded fragments of material caught up in its claws as it slashed and slashed again. Blood splattered the walls. Rosie's head lolled to one side, spared the sight and agony of that which was happening to her flesh as it was ripped from her bones. The crab slobbered as it sucked a string of her innards into its foul mouth.

It looked up, saw him and fixed its tiny, hate filled eyes on him. A shred of bloodied flesh slid from its mouth. There was no mistaking the threat from a raised pincer. You're next!

Donald recoiled, rushed back into the room, grabbed up the old 12-bore which stood in the corner. He opened the breech, inserted a couple of cartridges from those standing on the table. Heavy loads, buckshot.

"I'll fix you, you bastard!" He shouted.

On his return to the landing the crab was already half way up the stairs, a loathsome blood smeared devil from the deep, the last offspring of those giants which had taken their toll of human life around the globe. A survivor against all odds from the blast of an enemy bomb which had lain in wait for them for seven decades.

It was close and getting closer. Donald laughed hysterically as he cocked the hammers of his shotgun, aligned it from his hip the way he had seen gunfighters shoot in western movies.

A deafening, double explosion as both barrels detonated simultaneously. Twin stabs of flame, thick choking smoke filling the landing and stairway. Somewhere in the midst of that stinking, sulphurous cloud the crustacean would have been blasted to fragments.

Donald stood there, gave a shrill laugh.

Click–click–clickety–click.

Oh, Jesus God, I don't believe it!

The crab emerged from the smoke, hauled itself up on to the top step. Pieces were missing from its shot pitted shell but the head, that awful face, was unscathed.

Donald's mouth was wide, his cigarette bobbing up and down, affixed to his upper lip.

He leapt back, fled into the room which Rosie called his 'den', slamming the door behind him. It can't get me in here. Yes, it can, it smashed in the front door, didn't it?

And now it was determined to break down this one with mighty blows from its pincers, living battering rams which had already torn Rosie asunder.

A panel split and through the gap Donald glimpsed the crustacean. Its chilling threat had escalated to an uncontrollable fury. He had shot it, doubtless wounded it beneath its shell, and now it was crazy for revenge.

"Fuck off!" He yelled, reaching behind him for more cartridges. A dozen upright loaded tubes toppled over, rolled in all directions across the table top, thudded to the floor, rolled again.

"Fuck!"

A lower door panel splintered. A gap appeared, large enough for the crab to squeeze through.

Donald clambered up on to the table, stood at bay, wielding his unloaded gun like a club. A length of ash showered down his shirt front from that cigarette. Its tip glowed as he sucked in air.

The crab couldn't climb up the table the way it had ascended the stairs but it had other ideas. Pincers fastened on to a carved leg, shook it from side to side. The rickety structure creaked as it wobbled, almost toppled Donald from his precarious perch.

If only he had cartridges to reload the gun then at point-blank range he could surely blast his attacker into a heap of shell and shredded seafood. An idea, a last desperate throw of the dice. If he lay down on the flat surface, reached over the side furthest from his attacker, then maybe he could grab a cartridge before the crab grabbed him. It was worth a try.

Click–click–click

The bugger could read his thoughts but he managed to snatch a round off the floor ahead of a snapping pincer. The table shook, had him holding on desperately, head over the side. Any second he would be dislodged ...

He felt the cigarette coming free of his lip, sliding, falling in a shower of sparks, directly into the open tin of black gunpowder on the floor below.

The explosion was instantaneous, a blinding sheet of flame, the ceiling and the roof above disintegrating, debris flying in every direction, flames lighting up the night sky in a beacon of destruction and death.

Donald's corpse was tossed into the inferno, head hanging by a sinew as though in shame. Then it broke free bouncing onto the burning floor, striking a final blow on the dismembered crab before rolling through the doorway and coming to a halt at the top of the stairs.

The smouldering cranium looked down with dead eyes to where the rapidly blackening body of Rosie lay, spread-eagled in the hallway, crab chewed thighs wide. A final invitation to her husband.

The cottage shuddered as brickwork collapsed, the vibration caused Donald's head to start rolling again. A stair at a time, dull thud followed by dull thud, until the cracked, bloodied and blackened skull gyrated onto the ground floor. Rolling again, only coming to rest with tongue outstretched between the sizzling, parted thighs of his wife. Just one last time, Rosie. Please.

The stench of roasting crab meat drifted slowly down the stairway, mingling with the acrid powder smoke before dispersing through the smashed front door and out into the cold night air.

CRABS ARMARDA

Like the Spaniards of old, the Crab army massed to invade England

Boswell did not want to dive, the last thing he wanted was to go down into those green depths which became darker with every fathom until the only light you had to see by was the beam of your lamp.

His fears were illogical, he told himself that over and over again until he almost believed it. Because it was surely one of the easiest dives he had ever undertaken, the shipwreck was no more than twenty fathoms down. And that was the root of his fear.

The remnants of the Rata Encoronada had lain for four centuries out there in the Giant's Causeway, irrecoverable except at a cost which far out-weighed what was left of it. All the moveable treasures had been brought up, there was nothing worth going back down for. So the galleon had been left to rot on the ocean bed.

And now, suddenly, the wreck of the Spanish ship had moved to within a quarter of a mile of the shore line. An impossibility, except that it was right down there now.

The diver shuddered inside his wetsuit, hovered on the brink of a refusal, then pandered to his pride. There were many reasons he could have come up with for backing down at the last minute. I'm not feeling well, I've had this bout of flu hanging about for a couple of days. Why me, for Christ's sake? Because Arkwright's on vacation and I just happened to be around. In semi-retirement. The last time Boswell had dived had been when they were searching that loch for the body of a teenage girl who turned up very much alive with her boyfriend in Dublin three days later. A false alarm.

Come on, Boz, just an hour of your time. We want to know why the wreck has shifted. It had to be the tide that had dragged it. Nobody would believe that so the authorities wanted a diver to investigate. As if it bloody well mattered!

But right now it mattered a lot to Jack Boswell. A phenomena had occurred, something that defied the laws of the underwater, and he had to find out what.

Maybe twenty years ago he wouldn't have given it a second thought, he reflected as he slid over the side of the boat, gave one last upward envious glance at the lowering skies above. He was fifty now and a couple of decades had brought with it an attitude of caution which had been non-existent in 1968 when he had gone down to the wreck-site of the Girona. God, that had been the experience of a lifetime, he would never forget the thrill of handling those treasures, the ring of Thomas de Granvela's that had lain on the seabed for nearly four hundred years. The winching up of the cannons; press and television crews swarming around like vultures that had located a corpse in the desert. Like belated victory celebrations that had been kept on ice since 1588 and now it was finally time to gloat over the defeat of the Spanish Armada. Taking the credit for that which the raging seas had accomplished when, without the intervention of the elements, England would surely have fallen to the Spaniards. But that was all in the past.

Boswell experienced a sensation of weightlessness, a headiness brought on by the pressure of the water around him, usually a pleasant feeling but this time his flesh goose-pimpled. You're getting windy, Boz, a has-been giving it one last try just to prove something to yourself. The beam from his lamp cut a quivering swathe through the murkiness.

Gyrating, looking behind him in case something was sneaking up on him through the green tinged darkness. All you have to do is go and look, return and report ... what? A shipwreck just like any one of hundreds that littered the ocean beds around the globe. The treasures would be gone, just skeletons with their bones picked clean by ... Oh, Jesus Alive!

He came upon the shipwreck with frightening suddenness. He shied from it, back-pedalled instinctively because usually divers had to hunt for their destination. Afraid because it was in shallow water, because somehow it had travelled from right out there in the Causeway. And also because the galleon stood upright.

"The tides have lifted it", he spoke aloud inside his headpiece, "just as they dragged it here". A heap of rotting boards draped with aquatic vegetation tried to hide it. A load of scrap, driftwood that would be ripped asunder and floated ashore for the beachcombers to gather for kindling. He began to circle it warily.

The masts were long gone, small fish darted in and out of gaping holes, the portholes a myriad of dead eyes that watched his every move. Passing the captain's cabin, seeing how the gun-deck had collapsed, jettisoned its heavy cannons down to the bilge and the hold.

Boswell descended to the seabed, stood there looking. There was nothing obvious to explain why the Rata Encoronada had moved. Or why it rested in an upright position. He felt a stab of terror, an urge to flee for the surface, clamber aboard the waiting boat; to tell the others that there was nothing to see down there. But you haven't been gone long enough to find out, Boz. Get back down there and look again. Ten minutes, then, no longer. Another circle of the wreck, maybe a peek in through a porthole.

Academic, really, but having come this far he had to finish the job.

Something glinted in his lamp beam, had him edging towards the captain's cabin, curiosity temporarily overcoming his mounting fear. He focused his beam through the tentacles of floating seaweed, gasped in amazement. At first glance the object appeared to be a ten pence coin, which was bloody silly. He laughed inside his headgear and the sound frightened him because he recognised the beginnings of a hysteria which he was attempting to keep at bay. He shivered uncontrollably, it was so bloody cold down here.

Inside the cabin he knelt to pick up whatever it was, stared in disbelief at that which he held in his gloved hand. A tiny sundial made from pure silver. Now there was an element of excitement in his shaking. Small as it was, the thing had to be worth a fortune; it was in two pieces, came apart in his fingers. He found himself glancing around furtively as he slipped it into a small pouch pocket on his thigh. In all probability the others would not check him out with a metal detector, they had no reason to, because this galleon had been searched thoroughly the last time. Christ, his find might be worth a grand. Or two. Or five.

And that was the only reason why Boswell moved further into the wreck, all thoughts of a hasty return to the surface forgotten. The movement of the ship must have dislodged that sundial from wherever it had lain hidden, there could be other miniature treasures just for the taking. He laughed again and this time it did not scare him.

A skeleton with a broken rib cage grinned up at this intruder on the gun deck. Boswell stepped back, peered into the shadows in case there were others. He could not see any, did not look any further because his light had picked out something else on the slippery boards. He grabbed for it, afraid that it might somehow be whisked away from him, scooped it up greedily. A thimble, so small that he doubted whether it would have fitted his little finger. And for Boswell small was beautiful as he stuffed it into that pouch and checked to make sure that the sundial was still there.

There were more skeletons on the lower gun deck, it was only to be expected because this was where most of the sailors had lived during a long voyage. Perhaps these Spaniards had been sleeping when the Rata Encoronada was holed on the rocks, trapped down here when the water rushed in. There's no reason to stay any longer, Boz, you've got yourself a fortune. He turned away, checked that the bilge and the hold were directly below him. It would only take a few more minutes to check them out.

He shied away from a skeleton that sat propped in a corner, heard it yell 'thief' at him.

"Shut your mouth, you bastard!" He shouted back, almost deafened himself.

Thief ... bastard ... thief ... bastard ... thief ... The echoes vibrated his skull, had him trying to clutch his ears through his helmet. Steps above, steps below.

Boswell began the descent into the hold.

It was ten degrees colder in here than it had been outside on the seabed, he was sure of that. Impenetrably dark, his light struggled to illuminate the blackness. Just a wan beam that created grotesque moving shadows. He cowered. It was the marine vegetation wafting in the sluggish current like buntings in a breeze, reaching out, stretching to touch him. Boswell felt their slimy, icy fingertips stroking his back, whirled around and sent them entwined into temporary retreat. But others took him from behind, wrapped their ribbons around his arms and legs so that he had to tear himself free.

God, it was like a forest in here, a black hell hole where the weed was trying to smother him, hold him here for eternity so that his skeleton whitened alongside those of the Spanish sailors! He tore himself free, started to swim for that jagged hole that led up to the lower gun deck. And that was when his beam glinted on something that scintillated in the watery shadows.

Even in his terror he paused, trod water. His first thought was that it was a jewel, a gigantic sapphire that had eluded the original searchers. His heart skipped a beat. Jeez, there were two of them!

Staring in greed and disbelief, seeing how those things burned, glowed and dulled. And glowed again. Until finally he knew that they were no inanimate objects but pin-points that burned with living hatred and saw him! A pair of eyes that glittered in the blackness, and more behind them! And still more, like fiery stars lighting up a night sky.

Silhouettes were manifesting themselves in the swirling shadows, huge shells that hitherto had been part of the hold and bilge, monstrous shapes with extended pincers divesting themselves of their camouflage. Now Boswell saw their faces, the malevolent expressions and the pouted mouths, heard the clicking begin like faraway castanets growing in volume.

Click-click-clickety-click.

He heard himself screaming as he struck out for where his only escape route lay. Something hard brushed against him, buffeted him and knocked him off course; snapped shut within inches of his leg. Bone gnashing on bone, striking again in frustration and fury. He thought that his foot had gone but it was only his flipper, it made direction difficult like a fish that had lost a fin. Soaring sideways, seeing the exit he sought and missing it by a yard. Scrambling for it and seeing the crabs below him, his brain refusing to accept what his eyes showed him.

Crabs the size of farmyard cows, there must have been fifteen or twenty of them packed down in the hold, hiding from mankind. And now Boswell, the diver, had stumbled upon their lair and they were intent upon silencing him before he revealed their whereabouts to the world above the ocean!

Panicking because he was unable to locate the exit, dodging another claw, knowing that one small tear in his wetsuit would be equally as fatal as a decapitation. Eluding them because he was agile and they were cumbersome, but knowing that in the end their strength would wear him down. Perhaps it was better to surrender to them now and get it over with rather than prolong the inevitable.

Boswell grasped a beam to steady himself, a momentary rest, and that was when he felt the galleon move. He was almost dislodged, thought that perhaps the wreck had shifted in the current, unstable in its new resting place. Then he felt the timbers shudder, vibrate, was aware that the galleon was no longer stationary. And in that awful moment came the terrible realization of how the Rata Encoronada had travelled almost a mile along the bed of the Giant's Causeway towards the shore. The giant crabs had pushed it, dragged and carried it. Not only was the galleon their hideout, it was their warship en route to attack mankind!

The diver loosed his precarious hold, swam again in search of the hole that was his only hope but it was as though the rotting timbers had closed, an ancient trapdoor fallen to imprison him.

The crustaceans followed his progress, not hurrying, as though they sensed that he was their prey and that there was no escape for this trespassing human. Boswell saw their glowing eyes, magnified still further by the dark waters which their mutated bodies swirled, their cavernous mouths agape with lust for his flesh. He began to scream again.

The galleon was scraping, juddering its way along the seabed, lurching over rocks, gathering speed as though the spirits of the long-dead Thomas de Granvela and Don Alonso de Leyva were intent upon completing their mission of four centuries ago. They had called upon the crabs to conquer their enemies and capture the throne of England.

Finally, Boswell's strength failed him and as he made one last effort to elude those snapping pincers he knew that his legs were gone. Mercifully, he fainted before a claw disembowelled him and the crustaceans began to feast upon his mutilated body, slurping the entrails greedily and crunching the bones, quarrelling over the last morsels.

Afterwards, the Crabs' Armada continued on its direct course for the shoreline, fortified by its feast yet still hungering for human flesh and eager to launch an attack which had begun four hundred years earlier.

would never happen. I had a letter from h[...] is on the island of Tampini in the sou[...] between the lines, he has sunk to the[...] drinking himself to death."

"But you still want him bac[k]"

"I love him, Mister New[man] back I would insist upon too late."

Newman stretche[d...] beard.

"I have ne[ver] announced a[...] pipe. He [...] the fla[p...] the [...]

already [...] it meant working outsi[de...]

"You'd better fill me in on the detai[ls...] he was non-committal at this stage. He had embarked [...] a lifestyle deep in the countryside over the past five years and had a reluctance to disturb it. Money, though, would be the deciding factor.

"My family has owned the Keyland estate for two generations. I inherited it from my father some ten years ago and shortly afterwards I married Ralph. He was a fine man – until he took to the drink, steadily becoming an alcoholic. Of course, he relied on me for his income but after a time I had to curtail it. An upright man in every other way, guilt overcame him and he decided not to burden me with his problem any longer and left. With just a thousand pounds in his pocket he said that he was going to make his own way in life and when he had sorted himself out he would return and beg for forgiveness. An old and familiar story, I knew it

…im last week. He
…th seas and, reading
…lowest depths, steadily

…?"

…man. If I could only have him
…a course of treatment. Before it is

…d out his long legs and stroked his short

…er heard of the island of Tampini," he
…length, stuffing tobacco into a blackened briar
…id not ask her permission to smoke as he applied
…e of his lighter for this was his domain and he set
…les.

"I guess few people have," she gave a wry smile. "It's fairly sizeable and, I believe, still British, a throwback to the days of the Empire. A jewel set in a sapphire sea, but it is divided by complete contrasts, half is poverty stricken native shacks, the rest the ultimate in luxury. A divide of the rich and the poor. I dread to think in which area my Ralph is residing."

"I'll find him," Gary made an instant decision. It sounded a fascinating case. "And when I do, how do I get him back to England? Force or gentle persuasion?"

"I leave that up to you, Mister Newman," she opened her handbag, produced a photograph of a dapper man with a short-clipped moustache. "This is my husband … as he looked just after our marriage."

"Thank you," he stood up, a sign that their meeting was over. "I will make arrangements to go out to Tampini. I will, of course, keep you informed. Now, I must ask you for an advance on my fee. Shall we say two thousand pounds to cover travel and other expenses."

"That's fine by me," she opened her handbag again and took out a cheque book.

* * *

Gary booked in at the one and only hotel on Tampini, a shabby wooden building which bore signs of having been battered by numerous storms. It was apparent that there were no other guests staying there. The 'porter', an olive native wearing a grubby T-shirt and stained denim shorts, showed him to a ground floor room.

He set off on a tour of the sprawling shanty town, its streets still littered with debris from the last storm. Scantily clad natives were coming from the shore carrying fish which they had caught. The sea was the main source of sustenance for these people.

On a rise at the summit of the main thoroughfare was the police station, a single storey, squat edifice constructed of concrete blocks with just a couple of small windows overlooking the street.

Only one officer was on duty, clad in a crumpled uniform bearing the insignia 'police'. Overweight and eating a bowl of mixed gruel and fruit at the counter, he looked up as Gary entered.

"Can I help you?"

Gary introduced himself and briefly explained his mission which brought the hint of a smile to the officer's lips.

"Ralph Hildebrand," he spat out a melon pip into his bowl. "Everyone here knows Ralph. You'll find him in the gin hall down at the bottom of the street. He'll be drunk but that's the only time he's normal. When the booze runs out you won't get any sense out of him. I guess he'll run out of money before long and then there will be problems. You want to take him back to England, eh? No chance. The only way he'll go from the hall is when they carry him out in a wooden box. The boss lets him live in a shed at the back. Free of charge, of course, because his boozing pays for his keep. After that …"

"I'll give it a try," Newman smiled. "I have to start somewhere."

* * *

The gin hall was crowded, multi-national dropouts who had come to Tampini for a variety of reasons. Some were criminals who had fled their homelands, others bankrupts, and somewhere amongst them was Ralph Hildebrand.

"That's him over there in the corner," a Portuguese jerked a thumb, took another swig at the bottle in his hand. "He's sleeping it off right now. Best wait till he wakes up or you won't get any sense out of him. Sometimes he gets violent."

Ralph Hildebrand was virtually unrecognizable from the photograph which the detective carried in his wallet. His dark hair was now grey and his thick, unkempt beard straggled down his chest. He was clad in the remnants of the suit which he had been wearing on his arrival on Tampini. Bare flesh was visible through the frayed material of his trousers and a sole hung loose on a shoe.

"Jesus wept!" Gary lit his pipe, principally to mask the odour of sour sweat in this hovel. Nobody sat close to Hildebrand, even the natives gave him a wide berth.

Newman lowered himself on to a vacant chair. He would wait, however long it took. Those around took little notice of him, visitors to the island were of little interest.

After half-an-hour or so Hildebrand stirred. His eyes flickered open and he seemed confused. He shook his head, glanced around him and then his gaze settled on Gary.

"Who are you?" His speech was slurred.

"I'm Gary. I'm a friend of your wife's."

"Oh!" Ralph Hildebrand jerked into an upright sitting position.

"Why ... what are you doing here?"

"I've come a long way to find you, Ralph. I'm going to take you home. Back to the Keyland Estate and Maria."

"I'm not going home. Never!"

"I think you are, Ralph. There's a much better life waiting for you. You can't remain in this degradation, this hell, for the rest of your life. Your money's running out and Maria won't send you any more. What will you do then?"

"I'll just die. I let her down, I can't face her."

"She loves you, she wants you back. She'll fix your drink problem and then you'll be as you once were. And if you're embarrassed about having no income then there's a job awaiting you, managing the estate."

Ralph Hildebrand lapsed into silence. Gary waited patiently. It could be difficult from here on.

"I don't have the money to get home."

"I'll see to that. You'll come back with me."

Hildebrand closed his eyes. His alcohol numbed brain was struggling to come to terms with the offer.

"I'll have to think about it."

"Fair enough but right now you're coming back to the hotel with me. There's a comfortable bed in my room for you to rest on. We'll take it from there."

"All right." He tried to get up, fell back against the wall. Gary helped him up on to his feet, supported him. "Now, take it easy, a step at a time."

Outside the sky was beginning to cloud over and a stiff breeze was strengthening by the minute. A storm was brewing somewhere.

* * *

As Gary and Ralph emerged from the gin hall sudden chaos erupted along the entire length of the street. Crowds were running uphill, shouting, some falling and almost being trampled beneath a forest of feet. A uniformed policeman was perched upon a balustrade, shouting into a megaphone.

"Tsunami, tsunami!"

"Christ!" Gary pulled his companion back against the wall of a dowdy general store. "We'd better go to the police station, ask Inspector Tarnim what the hell's going on. There was no mention of a tsunami when I spoke to him earlier."

Hildebrand's expression was vague. He did not appear to understand, his alcoholic haze impervious to all that was happening around him. With no small amount of difficulty Gary dragged him along, negotiated his way through the onrushing, screaming, fleeing crowd.

Inspector Tarnim was clearly disturbed, shouting instructions to a couple of officers, frantically waving them out into the street.

"Oh, it's you!" He turned towards Gary. "I see you've found your friend Hildebrand. Drunk out of his mind as usual."

"What the hell's going on out there, Inspector?"

"Tsunami," the other replied. "Usually we get plenty of warning. Not this time, though. It'll hit the island in a couple of hours or so and it's huge according to information I've just received. People are panicking heading for the mountain, but there's always those reluctant to abandon their shacks down by the shore. They won't stand a chance."

"And the town?"

"Depends. It'll get up here, sixty foot waves and winds the likes of which you'll never've seen before. Most of the buildings have survived a few tsunamis in the past but some are getting pretty fragile. The police station will be ok, it's built of blocks and the doors and windows are sealed. The gin hall will go for certain and the hotel."

"Oh!" Gary's expression bordered on despair. He glanced at Hildebrand but the other did not seem to understand.

"So what do we do, Inspector?"

"Well ..." the officer grimaced. "Both the gin hall and the hotel will be crammed with folks who don't think it's vital to head for the mountain. There'll be casualties, nothing we can do about that, I'm afraid, and I'm certainly not having people in here shoulder to shoulder. Just police, there'll be more than enough for us to do after the storm has passed. Tell you what, you stop in here with that drunk of yours. You'll have to sleep on the floor in a cell but that's better than drowning."

"Thanks," Gary let out a sigh of relief. "I really do appreciate your offer."

"And you can help us afterwards," a wan smile, it wasn't just out of the kindness of the policeman's heart.

"There'll be corpses to be collected and taken to the mortuary. Mass graves. I don't expect Hildebrand will be much help but it might sober him up!" He gave a humourless laugh. "Go and fetch your things from the hotel whilst there's still time."

The wind was becoming stronger by the minute. A wooden hoarding crashed to the ground, cartwheeled and sent a fleeing native sprawling. He did not rise, lay slumped as numerous running feet trod on him.

* * *

"Here it comes!" Inspector Tarnim stood by a reinforced window, five officers crowding behind him. "God, the waves are up here already!"

The noise from the tearing gale and crashing waves made it virtually impossible for the occupants of the small police station to make themselves heard. A wall of foaming water hit the building; it vibrated but held firm. The expressions of the occupants were fearful. Nature was doing her damnedest to destroy Tampini.

Gary Newman watched from one of the water lashed windows. It was difficult to see beyond the foaming tide outside. Objects were thrown high. He thought some of them were human bodies.

A brief glimpse of a female running for her life. Gary saw her look over her shoulder just before she disappeared under a 20 foot wave. Dear God! He shuddered, no one could survive that.

More bodies. A strong male who had somehow managed to survive the initial surge of roaring sea water was attempting to secure a grip on an overhanging roof. The sheer force of the tsunami tore him free, tossed him, flung him against the side of the police station. His broken body continued on its way. Gary guessed that the man was probably dead by now, killed instantly on impact.

He turned away from the window. Ralph Hildebrand was slumped in a chair, seemed impervious to everything that was happening outside.

Gary wandered through to an adjoining room where an officer was in the process of boiling a kettle on a primus stove. The walls were shelved on one side, an array of items stacked on them, handguns, knives, packets that were undoubtedly prohibited drugs once intended for distribution by dealers.

"Confiscations from criminals," the young constable informed him, "they'll be destroyed, but there's more out there than in here. Or was. One good thing about this tsunami is that it'll destroy a load of outlawed stuff and," he grinned, "hopefully the crooks that sell them."

A resounding crash came from outside, one that even the height of the storm was unable to drown.

"That'll be the gin hall gone," the officer began pouring boiling water into mugs. "Good riddance, I say."

Gary accepted a couple of offered mugs of coffee, took one across to Hildebrand. The other took a sip.

"I guess you'll be accompanying me back to England after this lot's over Ralph."

Hildebrand's nod was in the affirmative. "I'll come with you. If we survive."

"Good." He returned to his vantage point at the window.

Hours passed.

"The tsunami's passing," Tarnim spoke after a long silence. "There will be floods that will take time to subside but up here it'll be no more than a few feet deep. There'll be corpses everywhere. Tomorrow we'll start the clear up. Relief will be arriving from the mainland."

Something attracted Gary's attention on the other side of the river-like street. Swirling debris, a body caught up in it, behind it something brownish and large. Somehow whatever it was seemed to be moving under its own strength, defying the current.

What the hell was it?

Then another similar partly submerged shape joined the first. A wave hid both temporarily then revealed them clearly.

There was no mistaking the shape of a crab, the shell and waving pincers.

"Come here and look at what's out there," he yelled to Inspector Tarnim. "Crabs ... as big as cows!"

The inspector was joined in his rush to the window by two other officers. All stared in disbelief.

"They're crabs, all right," Tarnim's dark complexion had paled. "And there's more over there!"

"It's impossible!"

"Improbable, not impossible. Forty years ago big buggers like those out there made world headlines attacking the UK's coast. Then they turned up on the Great Barrier Reef. Created, so it was believed, by some kind of underwater nuclear test which mutated them. Then in other places. The authorities thought that they had finally exterminated them. Obviously they hadn't and the survivors have been hiding out on the ocean bed – until the force of this tsunami washed 'em up here!"

"Oh, my God!" Gary almost threw up. The crabs were hunting for corpses of drowned humans. One had a slim woman gripped in a pincer, crushed the body so that it opened up, exuding blood and entrails. Nearby another crustacean was devouring the flesh of a male who was still in the last throes of life.

More crabs followed. The banquet of human bodies was just beginning.

"There's rifles in the armoury," Gary had noticed some half-a-dozen in a rack beside the shelving.

"I don't think they'd be much use even at point-blank range," Tarnim answered. "They're ex-army .303s from the First World War, all that the powers that be would supply us with along with shotguns for riot control. We don't even have grenades, not that they'd be much use either."

More debris floated with the raging tide, amidst which was a sign in faded paint announcing 'Hotel.' Gavin's stomach muscles tightened. If he and Ralph had sought refuge in his former accommodation then their bodies would probably have been out there on the crab's menu.

"Now they've found humans to feed on, God alone knows when we'll ever be rid of them," Tarnim groaned, "and it won't be safe to go out there. We're trapped in here, Mister Newman!"

Gary wandered back into the store room which doubled as a kitchen. Idly his gaze followed along the shelves, the weaponry, the drugs. A glass jar caught his eye, it had a handwritten label on it.

"Inspector," he went to the doorway, shouted. Tarnim came across the main office, that worried expression seemingly engraved upon his features.

"There's more of the bastards out there," he grunted. "Maybe a dozen and Christ knows how many more there are that we can't see. We'll soon know when the water subsides!"

"Just curious," the detective reached the glass jar down from the shelf. "How is it you've got a quantity of strychnine in here?"

"Oh, that!" Tarnim replied. "It's been there for years. I confiscated it from a peasant farmer in the hills. He was using it to bait and kill seabirds which were taking eggs from his poultry. A banned substance these days, for use only under licence and he certainly wouldn't be granted one. Why do you ask?"

"I've got the germ of an idea," Gary mused.

He returned to his vantage point at the window, steeled himself to watch what was happening outside.

Within a couple of hours the storm had abated somewhat, just a howling gale which continued to fling debris in all directions. A broken door from one of the buildings further down hit the steel grid which protected the police station window, splintered into fragments. The water level in the street had dropped to about a couple of feet but was still churning and frothing. He counted five giant crabs out there, all frenziedly tearing at floating corpses, an unprecedented choice of food for these monsters which the tsunami had hurled ashore from their ocean refuge.

Bile scorched in his throat. A crab had grabbed a floating man by the leg, pulled him close. The amputation was instant; the body began to drift away with the current. A swift grab caught an arm, dragged it close, pinned it below the surface of the water. The corpse was ripped open from groin to throat and then another unholy feast began. Entrails resembling a nest of eels were sucked into the creature's mouth. Its very posture denoted delight.

Gary knew what he had to do, the very thought was sickening. He returned to the store, searched along the shelves. His fingers closed over the container labelled 'strychnine.' He also took a Browning .38 automatic pistol with a full ammunition clip alongside it. He snapped it loaded, found a 6-inch sheathed knife further down and slipped it on his belt. He made his way back to the main office.

"What're you doing with those?" Inspector Tarnim turned away from the window.

"I'm going out there. The water level's below the steps. Open the door and shut it after me."

"You're crazy!"

"Maybe but it's our only chance, and that of any inhabitants of the town who are still alive."

"A .38 won't even tickle a crab."

"Agreed but I feel better with one in my hand as well as this." He held up the glass jar, shook the white granules inside it. "It's a long shot but I'm going to try it."

"All right," Tarnim nodded, he did not even ask what Gary's plan was, he was a dead man walking. He shot back the bolts on the door, "it's been nice knowing you, Mister Newman."

On the chair in the corner Ralph Hildebrand stared fixedly ahead of him with glazed eyes. He didn't understand, perhaps it was better that way.

The wind buffeted Gary, it was all he could do to keep his balance. A glance up the street revealed that the crabs' feeding frenzy was still by the wreck of the gin hall. A severed, bearded head floated away from the scene; a skull had little in the way of edible offerings for these scavengers from the sea.

The girl caught up on the overturned car had her thighs open at full stretch, her knees slightly bent. Gary swallowed as he waded out to her, sick to his stomach because he knew what he had to do, the most revolting act of his life.

He slipped the knife from its leather sheath, tested the blade carefully with his thumb. The steel had been honed to razor sharpness which would aid the gruesome task which he was about to perform.

He bent over her, whispering under his breath, "I'm so sorry, forgive me." Some hours before, this young woman had a life, maybe a family. He struggled to push these thoughts from his mind.

The blade cut deep and easily. He made three cuts six inches long, horizontally across her belly. The wounds were deep enough for the purpose but not enough to let the contents spill from the body.

He wiped the blade clean and returned it to its sheath. Now the jar of strychnine, having to use force to free the screw top. He shook some of the granules out, spreading them liberally in every wound. Those greedy bastards would feast on the girl without suspicion.

Glancing about him he could see the crabs still feeding on the corpse by the gin hall. There were none close by. Thank God!

Another human corpse caught his eye, half submerged but pinned by his legs beneath a heavy oak beam. The man's clothing was torn apart, exposing enough bare flesh for Gary Newman's purpose.

He retched again as he cut into the man. He thought for one awful moment that the other was still alive but movements of the arms were only due to the current. Once again he baited the wounds with a liberal dose of strychnine.

Taking a risk he worked quickly on one other body, praying that the monsters would all share in the feast that Gary had prepared for them. His father had once told him that a single grain was enough to kill an adult. The crabs would have a generous helping, he hoped it would be sufficient.

He tossed the bloody, slimy knife away, swilled his hands in the water. He tried to take control of his shuddering body.

Then out came the Browning. Five shots at those feeding crabs, the bullets ricocheting off the huge shells like peas from a kid's pea-shooter. The crustaceans heard the strikes rather than felt them. Three turned towards the source of this annoyance, strings of scavenge trailing from their mouths.

The sheer audacity of human retaliation would bring them down to the poisoned bait surely.

Tarnim eased the door open at Gary's approach, held it whilst the detective squeezed inside, slammed it shut after him and shot the bolts home.

"Thank God you made it! Well?"

"The poison bait is laid," Gary felt physically sick still. "All we need now is for the bastards to come and eat it. Unless they decide to head on uphill after live victims."

"Don't be negative. All we can do is wait and see."

"It'll be dark soon. Night comes fast here. We won't know anything until morning."

"Then we'll try to get some sleep and review the situation by daylight."

Ralph Hildebrand was on his feet, holding on to the chair for support. "When are we going back to England?" He asked with a shaky voice.

"Soon," Gary answered. At least there was a small bonus to the coming of the crabs.

* * *

Morning.

Tarnim and his officers were already at the window when Gary came through to the reception area.

"Not a sign of a crab," the inspector shook his head. "Just wreckage and mutilated bodies out there."

"Then we'd better go and take a look. There'll surely be tracks which will tell us in which direction they've gone, uphill or back to the shore. Strychnine kills fast, so my Dad used to say, but here we're dealing with massive creatures. It may be some time before the poison kicks in."

Tarnim followed Gavin outside. Buildings which still stood were badly damaged, some roofless. They had to pick their way carefully through the wreckage.

"Look, there's claw prints," Gary pointed to a deep scrapes on the tarmac. "And there's others, heading back to the shore."

There were more marks, but no sign yet of a dead crustacean. Down below lay the beach, still awash from the tsunami like a flooded marsh although the tide had receded. There was debris from buildings, uprooted trees, a scene of devastation.

"There's a crab!" Tarnim shouted, pointing to a shape out on the mud. "And it looks pretty dead to me."

The beach was churned up, irregular furrows, crazy tracks all heading seawards as if the crabs were drunk, like Ralph Hildebrand.

"They certainly weren't feeling in the best of health," Gary grinned, light relief after all the recent horrors. "Like a drunken army in retreat, following an instinct which led them back to their ocean homeland."

"There's one lying in the edge of the water. And another further down from it. How many there were we'll never know but one thing's certain, they ate the bodies with the strychnine in. And doubtless there will be more crab corpses lying at various intervals in the sea as they struggled to make their way back to wherever they've been hiding."

"You've done a good job, Mister Newman." Praise from Inspector Tarnim was praise indeed.

"Let's hope so," Gary turned away. "Now my next move is to get Hildebrand back to England."

"There will be relief starting to arrive later today. Doctors, medical supplies and food, volunteers helping the survivors and trying to find any still alive who are buried beneath the rubble of collapsed buildings. It'll be a long job. Hopefully you'll get a lift back to the mainland on a relief helicopter's return trip. They usually fly to and fro in relays."

Ralph Hildebrand was waiting for their return in the doorway of the police station, a sobered wreck of a man, a shadow of his former self. "I need a drink," he greeted them.

"I'll make you a coffee," Gavin replied, tight-lipped, "and you're staying right by my side until we get back to your wife. No vodka, whisky or any other alcohol will pass your lips in the meantime."

Gary looked back, saw the sparkling blue sea in the distance, hardly a ripple on its surface. The tsunami had been and gone, left a trail of death and destruction in its wake.

It had also been instrumental in the extermination of the giant crabs which had survived for four decades. Gone forever. At least he hoped so.

ABOUT THE AUTHOR

I had my first story published in a local newspaper at the age of 12, followed by 55 more before I was 17. It was a good start to a writing career and I owe much of it to my mother (historical novelist E.M. Weale) who gave me every encouragement. My father, though, was insistent that I followed family tradition and went into banking.

Hence it was twenty years later before I became a full-time author and I had some catching up to do. The 1970's were a boom time for pulp fiction and I made my debut with 'Werewolf by Moonlight' (NEL 1974). It was 'Night of the Crabs', though, which really established me as a writer, virtually overnight in that memorable record, hot summer of 1976. This title was the 'No.1 beach read'. It saw numerous reprints, spawned 6 sequels along with several short stories, as well as a movie.

'Night of the Crabs' enabled me to go full-time. At the time with my wife, Jean, and our four children we were living a reasonably conventional life in Tamworth, Staffordshire. It was time to move on though, and in 1977 we moved to our present home in a remote part of the Shropshire/Welsh border hills.

I was no stranger to country life though, and the further away we were from town and traffic the better. For many years I had been writing for the 'Shooting Times' and several other sporting publications. Then in 1999 I accepted the post of Gun Editor of 'The Countryman's Weekly'. This involved 4-5 articles per week and I relished the challenge.

By this time pulp fiction was virtually out of fashion so diversification suited me, yet my readership has remained faithful to me and technology has made it all possible again with e-books. Thus my backlist is completely returned to electronic print along with some new books. It is an exciting time.

BIBLIOGRAPHY

Werewolf series

- Werewolf by Moonlight (1974)
- Return of the Werewolf (1976)
- The Son of the Werewolf (1978)

Crab series

- Night of the Crabs (1976)
- Killer Crabs (1978)
- The Origin of the Crabs (1979)
- Crabs on the Rampage (1981)
- Crabs' Moon (1984)
- Crabs: The Human Sacrifice (1988)
- Killer Crabs: The Return (2013)
- Crabs Omnibus (2015)

Truckers series

- The Truckers 1: The Black Knights (1977)
- The Truckers 2: Hi-Jack! (1977)

Sabat series

- Sabat 1: The Graveyard Vultures (1982)
- Sabat 2: The Blood Merchants (1982)
- Sabat 3: Cannibal Cult (1982)
- Sabat 4: The Druid Connection (1983)
- Dead Meat (1996) (omnibus of all 4 books plus two new Sabat stories, Vampire Village and Hellbeat)

Thirst series

- Thirst (1980)
- Thirst II: The Plague (1987)

Deathbell series
- Deathbell (1980)
- Demons (1987)

Sucking Pit series
- The Sucking Pit (1975)
- The Walking Dead (1984)

Slime Beast Series
- The Slime Beast (1975)
- Spawn of the Slime Beast (2015)

Written as Gavin Newman
- The Hangman (1994)
- An Unholy Way to Die (1999)

Other Fiction Titles
- Der Ruf des Werwolfs (1976) (Originally printed in German only, Published by Erich Pabel as a part of their "Vampir Horror Roman")
- The Ghoul (1976) (film novelization)
- Bamboo Guerrillas (1977)
- Bats Out of Hell (1978)
- Locusts (1979)
- Satan's Snowdrop (1980)
- Caracal (1980)
- Doomflight (1981)
- Warhead (1981)
- Entombed (1981)
- Manitou Doll (1981)
- Wolfcurse (1981)
- The Pluto Pact (1982)
- The Lurkers (1982)
- Blood Circuit (1993)

- The Undead (1983)
- Accursed (1983)
- Throwback (1985)
- The Wood (1985)
- Abomination (1986)
- The Neophyte (1986)
- Snakes (1986)
- Cannibals (1986)
- Alligators (1987)
- Bloodshow (1987)
- Fiend (1988)
- The Island (1988)
- The Master (1988)
- The Camp (1989)
- The Festering (1989)
- Mania (1989)
- Phobia (1990)
- The Unseen (1990)
- Carnivore (1990)
- The Black Fedora (1991)
- The Resurrected (1991)
- The Knighton Vampires (1993)
- Witch Spell (1993)
- The Plague Chronicles (1993)
- The Dark One (1995)
- Dead End (1996)
- Water Rites (1997)
- The Pony Riders (1997)
- The Busker (1998)
- Deadbeat (2003)
- Blackout (2006)
- The Cadaver (2007)
- Maneater (2009)

- Nightspawn (2010)
- The Eighth Day (2012)
- Psalm 151 (2013)
- Hangman's Hotel and other stories (2014)

Children's Books Written as Jonathan Guy

- Cornharrow (1988)
- Badger Island (1993)
- Rak: The Story of an Urban Fox (1994)
- Pyne (1995)
- Hawkwood (1996)
- The Minster Geese (2013)

Non-Fiction

- Gamekeeping and Shooting for Amateurs (1976)
- Tobacco Culture: A DIY Guide (1977)
- Ferreting and Trapping for Amateur Gamekeepers (1978)
- Hill Shooting and Upland Gamekeeping (1978)
- Profitable Fishkeeping (1979)
- Ratting and Rabbiting for Amateur Gamekeepers (1979)
- Sporting and Working Dogs (1979)
- Animals of the Countryside (1980)
- Moles and Their Control (1980)
- The Rough Shooter's Handbook (1986)
- Practical Country Living (1988)
- Writing Horror Fiction (1996)
- Hunting Big Cats in Britain (2000)
- Pipe Dreams an Autobiography (2013)

Printed in Great Britain
by Amazon